Moose,

the Thing, and Me

Moose,

the Thing,

and Me

William E. Butterworth

Houghton Mifflin Company   Boston   1982

Library of Congress Cataloging in Publication Data

Butterworth, W. E. (William Edmund), 1929–
  Moose, the thing, and me.

  Summary: Things are wild enough at the Ludwell School
before Moose Hanrahan's arrival, but Moose's incredible
size adds an entirely new dimension to school hijinks.
  [1. School stories.   2. Humorous stories]   I. Title.
PZ7.B9825Mn   1982   [Fic]   82-11730
ISBN 0-395-32077-1

Printed in the United States of America
V 10 9 8 7 6 5 4 3 2 1

Moose,

the Thing, and Me

Chapter 1

The last thing I expected to see when Number Three and I went back to our cell at the orphanage was a long-haired blonde lady sitting on my bed staring at my stuffed owl.

For one thing, long-haired blonde ladies aren't very often seen at the orphanage, period. And for another, there are very few people at the orphanage, even longtime inmates, who know how to find our cell. Number Three, The Thing, and I share accommodations on the fourth floor (in other words, in what used to be the attic) of Foxcroft Hall. Access to our home-away-from-home is via a staircase so steep it's more like a ladder, conveniently hidden behind a door off the third-floor corridor.

We live, we like to think, in solitary splendor, far above the common herd of inmates in the cells on the lower floors. We seldom have unexpected visitors. For one thing, the stairway is so steep and narrow that the live-in guards really have to be inspired with a sense of duty to come up and have a look at us. More important than that when it comes to discouraging visitors, when you get right down to it, is The Thing. The Thing looks like your ordinary, run-of-the-mill Old English sheepdog. That is, he weighs about 125 pounds, including about five pounds of ten-inch-long fur. He looks as lovable and roly-poly as the relatives of his you see all the time on TV, gulping down one brand of dog food or another.

But unlike his cousins in the TV profession, The Thing is not what you really could call a friend of man. The only reason The Thing hasn't bitten more people than he has is that even the none-too-bright inmates understand the message he's giving when he curls his lips back, makes bloodcurdling noises in his chest, and shows off about three pounds of teeth. The only reason The Thing doesn't bite Number Three and me is that we have known him since he was a pup. When The Thing was nothing more than an adorable bundle of fur, weighing, at three months, no more than forty pounds, he bit me. I was so astonished at this unprovoked attack from an animal for whom I had risked the wrath of the orphanage in getting him things to eat from the kitchen that I did the only thing that came to mind. I bit him back. That was the first and last time The Thing tried to bite me.

In the next couple of months, before Number Three came around to understanding that the only way to deal with The Thing was to think and act like a dog, The Thing made Number Three's life miserable. I really think that Number Three would still be sleeping on the floor, while The Thing slept in his bed, if The Thing hadn't gone too far. One morning The Thing woke up, looked down at the floor, and saw not only that Number Three was sound asleep, but that that part of him on which he sits was both out from under the blanket and out from under his pajamas. The Thing nipped him, playfully but enthusiastically, just barely hard enough to draw a little blood. Then, delighted with the noise Number Three was making, he sat down to see what was going to happen next.

Number Three did the only thing he could think of under the circumstances. The Thing was by then already too big to wrestle to the floor and bite, so Number Three couldn't use my solution to the problem. Instead, he threw my stuffed owl at him.

I inherited my stuffed owl from my paternal grandfather. Grandfather is an owl fancier. He believes that our founding fathers made a serious mistake when they picked the bald eagle to be our national emblem. According to Grandfather, the bald eagle is, compared to the owl, a really stupid bird. As strange as this might sound, it makes more sense to me than going along with Benjamin Franklin. The Father of American Independence thought that the turkey should be our national bird. Can you imagine that? Twice a year, at Thanksgiving and Christmas, people all over the country would sit down and eat the national emblem.

Anyway, Grandfather is an owl fancier. He must have ten of them, stuffed, sitting around on top of cabinets in his apartment in the Athletic Club. When I asked for one, he gave me the pride of his collection. My mother said he did it just to make her mad. My owl is a huge one, with eyes the size of a half-dollar. It was stuffed with its wings extended.

Old English sheepdogs, with all that hair hanging over their eyes, don't see too well. When Number Three threw my stuffed owl at him, The Thing didn't really know what hit him. One moment he was sitting there, playing with Number Three, and the next moment an enormous bird comes flying through the air to hook its beak in his fur and hang on for dear life. The Thing, even then, was pretty smart for a dog. He ran under the bed. When he did that, my stuffed owl got knocked loose. I ran over and grabbed the owl before The Thing could figure out that it really wasn't chasing him. I put it back on the bookshelf.

The Thing hid under the bed for about thirty minutes. Every time he stuck his nose out, he could look up and see the owl sitting there, looking at him out of those big yellow eyes, just waiting for a chance to attack. The way The Thing came to look at it, it didn't make any sense to bite Number Three anymore. There were a lot of other people around he could bite — people who didn't have vicious owls to defend them.

The third reason that we seldom get any visitors in our cell, in addition to the steep stairway and The Thing, is because of Number Three. It's what is known as guilt by association. Number Three's father, James Foxcroft Ludwell, Jr., is our warden. His father, J. Foxcroft Ludwell, Sr., was the founder of the Ludwell School. Number Three is officially James Foxcroft Ludwell III, but everybody except his parents calls him Number Three.

It isn't really an orphanage. In fact, one of the best ways to get in trouble with James Foxcroft Ludwell, Jr., is to let him hear you refer to the Ludwell School as The Orphanage. Next best is to let him hear you refer to the resident faculty as the Live-In Guards.

That makes him almost as mad as when somebody slips and lets him hear us call ourselves the inmates.

What the Ludwell School is, according to the catalogue, is "a high school and home for young gentlemen who for some reason cannot live with their families." What this means, generally, is that our parents have gotten divorced and sometimes remarried, and that we don't get along with the person they are now married to. So, to keep everybody happy, we are shipped off to the Ludwell School, where our "characters are molded in a disciplined yet homelike atmosphere, to promote academic excellence and prowess on the athletic fields."

Junior Ludwell takes the catalogue seriously, especially that part about "prowess on the athletic fields." I looked up "prowess" in the dictionary. It means "valor," "bravery," "gallantry," and "material daring." Number Three and I are big disappointments to Junior Ludwell in the prowess department.

In fact, one of the main reasons Number Three lives in Foxcroft Hall with me is his lack of prowess on the athletic fields. Junior Ludwell decided a couple of years ago, when he found out that Number Three not only hadn't made the Ludwell Lions Junior Varsity but hadn't gone out for it, that Number Three was not in the "Ludwell Mainstream." What he meant by this was that Number Three was still living at home, in what they call Headmaster's House.

What had really happened was that Number Three had figured out, about the same time that I had figured out, that football is a great game if you happen to have the build of a gorilla. Since Number Three and I are not built like gorillas, we had proceeded logically to the next truth: The reason the gorillas encourage small people to go out for football is so that they will have somebody to walk on.

Junior Ludwell decided that the way to get Number Three out on the football field was to submerge him in the Ludwell Mainstream — that is, move him out of Headmaster's House and into Foxcroft Hall. In Foxcroft Hall, Number Three would surely be inspired by what they call peer-group pressure to rush right out on the football field and get stepped on.

Junior Ludwell underestimated his son and namesake. Number Three wouldn't have gone out for football if they had burned him in effigy. It was at this point, although I had known Number Three for years, that we became friends. What happened was that the peer-group pressure they decided to apply to Number Three was to move him in with me. I had already demonstrated what Coach Ramsey called "an absolutely un-American and disgusting lack of school football spirit." My lack of spirit had seen me banished to the attic of Foxcroft Hall. The original idea was that I would have time, up there all alone, to reconsider my position and make a sacrifice of myself, to be stepped on by the gorillas.

When Number Three refused to go out for football, too, he was moved in with me. While I really have no idea how the mind of a football coach works, I suppose the idea was that if there were two of us banished to the attic, we would be twice as ashamed of ourselves for our un-American and disgusting lack of school football spirit.

Of course, it didn't work out that way. So far as Number Three and I were concerned, we were a faint candle of sanity burning in the dark. And, of course, The Thing, once he came to live with us, had a lot to do with keeping peer-group pressure down to a point where we could live with it. The Thing likes footballs. Not the game of football. The inflated leather obloids they play the game with. The Thing likes nothing better than to catch one and eat it. He especially likes the hissing noise it makes when he first sinks his fangs in it.

When Number Three and I climbed the narrow flight of stairs and found the blonde lady sitting on my bed staring at my stuffed owl, The Thing wasn't with us. As on every Visitor's Day, which this was, or when other schools were visiting us, The Thing was locked up. There is a storage room, with concrete block walls and a steel door, in the Alfred J.

MacNeeley Memorial Field House. First thing in the morning, whenever there are going to be visitors on the campus, Number Three and I have a sacred responsibility. We have to entice The Thing into the storeroom and lock him up. The storeroom is the only place that will hold him.

There have been incidents which have made this necessary. For some reason, when the inmates write home, they seem to give mothers and stepmothers (who seem to worry about this sort of thing) the impression that they are being systematically starved to death in the dining hall. The result of this is that most mothers or stepmothers, when they come to visit their inmates, often bring some really fancy picnic lunches, to be eaten on what the catalogue calls our "verdant, tree-shaded campus."

The Thing can't really be blamed for what happened. He had learned that when he went to the dining-hall kitchen door and barked, Mr. Abraham Lincoln O'Malley, our executive chef, could be counted on to give him a bone or something. Mr. O'Malley is sort of our resident rustic philosopher. He says, "Dogs you feed bite you less often than dogs you don't, especially big hairy ones like that Thing."

What happened was that The Thing, who can smell something to eat three miles away, sniffed his way to a picnic table where a stepmother was slicing a roast turkey. If she had given him a piece of skin or something when The Thing barked at her, he would have gone away happy, and that would have been the end of it.

But she didn't. I don't know whether she had never had a dog that large bark at her before or what, but what she did when The Thing asked for a little something to eat, as politely as he knew how, was climb up on the picnic table and start screaming. She was a little stout, even considering some of our other stepmothers, and when she got up on the picnic table, one of the legs sank into the grass. The stepmother and the turkey wound up on the ground. The Thing was by now, understandably, a little confused. He didn't have very much experience with screaming women, and this one could have been an opera singer, to judge by the noise she was making. So he did the perfectly natural thing for him to do under the circumstances. He grabbed the turkey in his mouth and lit out for our cell.

Number Three's mother, also known as Junior's Mate, got us out of that one. She flatly refused to believe that Number Three's darling little puppy dog (she hadn't seen The Thing in six months; Junior's Mate is allergic to dogs) was the ferocious snarling monster the stepmother said he was. And her little darling was simply incapable of training a dog to attack innocent women, as the stepmother accused.

It wasn't until The Thing interrupted morning worship services that Junior Ludwell put his foot down and came out with the ultimatum that either The Thing got locked up when there were visitors on the campus or he would ship The Thing out to Colorado where some Ludwell School alumnus was in the sheep-ranching profession.

The Ludwell School is nondenominational. What that means is that we have a steady procession of visiting clergymen of various religious persuasions who conduct worship services either in the Portman T. Danwood Memorial Nondenominational Chapel, or, when the weather is right, at the Outdoor Chapel at the edge of the lake. The Outdoor Chapel is a bunch of folding chairs set up on the grass.

I don't remember what persuasion that particular clergyman was, but I remembered him from a previous visit as being one of the enthusiastic, arm-waving types. He had a purple robe with billowing sleeves. He also led the hymn-singing. He was a lot like Coach Ramsey giving one of his pep talks to the Ludwell Lions.

About a quarter of the way through the service, after the opening hymn-singing (which woke The Thing up and brought him over to see what was happening) and during the first part of the praying, The Thing appeared in the Outdoor Chapel. He ambled slowly down the aisle between the folding chairs to the front. He's a dog, so he obviously didn't know what was going on, but he saw all of us paying attention to the reverend, and he apparently decided he would see what the reverend was up to. He lay down with his head on his paws and was quiet while the reverend finished his praying.

Then came the sermon. The reverend marched up close to the first row of chairs and looked around the congregation as if he wanted to make sure everybody was awake. The Thing raised his head and looked over his shoulder where the reverend was looking. Somebody giggled, and the reverend turned his head and gave him a dirty look, and then he saw The Thing.

You could tell he didn't like it much, and I had the idea that he was considering just what he should do about it. I suppose he wasn't used to having dogs at services he conducted, but on the other hand, I suppose he didn't have much experience running worship services on the grass, either. He apparently decided that the best thing to do was nothing — to get on with the sermon. He looked around the congregation again, as if checking to make sure nobody had gone to sleep during the praying, and then swung into his sermon.

The reverend raised both arms, wrapped in those enormous purple sleeves, over his head. "My friends!" he boomed. And then he stopped.

The Thing was on his feet, showing the reverend all of his teeth and giving out one of his growls. If Sir Arthur Conan Doyle had ever heard The Thing growl, that book would be called *The Sheepdog of the Baskervilles*. And this was one of The Thing's more sincere growls: The way the reverend's billowing purple sleeves were flapping around his head, The Thing thought it was another owl about to attack. He had already had a bad experience with one owl, and he was prepared to defend himself this time.

Very slowly, the reverend lowered his arms. And very slowly, The Thing stopped growling, stopped showing his teeth, and sat down on his haunches.

"My friends," the reverend began again, very slowly, this time with his arms held close to his sides. I don't remember what that particular sermon was all about, to tell you the truth. I was devoting most of my attention to The Thing. But I do remember what happened. A couple of minutes into the sermon the reverend got carried away with what he was saying. First, the way they all seem to, he started talking louder, and then he began waving his arms around, for emphasis.

Right in the middle of saying something about the wages of sin, he stopped. The Thing was on his feet again. Actually, it looked more as if he was walking on his tiptoes. If you've ever seen two dogs trying to decide who gets the one bone they've found — the way they walk around it, and each other, showing their teeth — you'll have an idea of how it was between the reverend and The Thing.

The Thing absolutely did not attack the reverend, no matter what the reverend thought or told Junior Ludwell later. He just started walking toward the reverend, and the reverend just started walking backward, and the first thing you know there he was in the lake, which is about eight feet deep at that point. As Number Three and I told Junior Ludwell if The Thing had really wanted to attack the reverend, he would have gone right in the lake after him instead of just standing at the edge of the water barking cheerfully as half of the football team hauled the reverend out.

But, as I say, it was what Junior Ludwell called an unfortunate incident, and both Number Three and I knew that he meant what he said about one more unfortunate incident and off The Thing would go to Colorado and the Ludwell alumnus in the sheep-ranching profession.

Later, Number Three found out from his mother that it could have been worse. Junior Ludwell was really on the reverend's side about the whole thing until the reverend got carried away again when explaining to his wife over the telephone why she had to come out to the Ludwell School with some dry clothes for him. He told his wife, forgetting for the moment that Junior Ludwell could hear him, that it was just the sort of thing you would expect at a school where the chapel was named after you-know-who. What the reverend was making reference to was that the Portman T. Danwood Memorial Non-denominational Chapel had been given to the school by Portman T. Danwood, Jr., class of '39, in memory of his father, who was president of the Kentucky Sour-Mash Bourbon Distillery, Inc. Not only did the Danwood family loyally support the Ludwell School during its annual fund-raising, but regularly as clockwork they sent Junior Ludwell a case of Danwood's Guaranteed Sour-Mash Dew at New Year's, for medicinal purposes, and Junior Ludwell was not about to listen to any criticism of such loyal alumni from anybody.

Chapter 2

As I said, Number Three and I were so surprised to find anybody in our cell, much less a blonde lady who looked (except that she had her clothes on) like those ladies in the fold-out pages of those magazines we were absolutely forbidden to read, that we were speechless.

She wasn't.

"Hi, there," she said, getting up from the bed. She walked over to Number Three and pinched his cheek. "I would have known you anywhere!"

"You would have?" Number Three asked.

"You look just like your daddy!" she said.

"I do?" Number Three said. He was sort of surprised by that. Number Three takes after his mother. That is, he's tall and skinny. Junior Ludwell, who he was supposed to look just like, is about five foot three and weighs 230 pounds.

"And your daddy has been looking *all* over for you!" the blonde lady said. *"Wherever* have you and your little friend *been?"*

Frankly, that question worried me. Junior Ludwell, on Visitor's Day, never goes looking for Number Three. He confers with parents and/or guardians on Visitor's Day. Conferring with parents and/or guardians means that he stands with a friendly arm draped around the inmate's shoulders, encouraging him to tell his parents and/or guardians how happy he is here at the Ludwell School. If Junior Ludwell was looking for Number Three, that probably meant he suspected that Number Three and I had not spent Visitor's Day engaging in what the catalogue called "supervised recreational activities."

In other words, neither Number Three nor I wanted to tell the blonde lady, who talked like she was running out of breath, where we had been.

Fortunately, Number Three never had time to answer the question, for at that moment my father appeared, a little out of breath himself after having climbed three flights of stairs and the ladder to our cell.

"As much as it costs me to keep you in this place," my father greeted me, "I don't understand why they make you live in the attic. How are you, Rutherford?"

"*He's* little Rutherford?" the blonde lady asked.

"Couldn't you tell?" my father said. "Everybody says he looks just like me."

"Of *course* I could," the blonde lady said. "I could tell the *moment* I *saw* him." She let go of Number Three and started over to me. I knew that she was going to pinch my cheek if I gave her half a chance, so I quickly picked up my stuffed owl and started stroking its feathers. It worked. She stopped about four feet away and contented herself with flashing me a dazzling smile. She had a lot of teeth.

"Rutherford," my father said. "This is Miss Lewis. Miss Amanda Lewis."

"How do you do?" I said.

"Your *daddy* and I," Miss Amanda Lewis said, flashing me another toothpaste-commercial smile, "wanted *you* to be the *first* to *know*."

"To know what?" I inquired.

"Amanda and I are going to be married," my father said.

"Aren't you *thrilled?*" Miss Amanda Lewis inquired.

To tell the truth, I wasn't exactly thrilled. What I was was surprised.

My father, like my grandfather Peters, is in the construction business. Mostly dams and roads, not houses. I wondered where he had met Miss Amanda Lewis. She didn't look like the ladies you saw around construction projects, but she didn't look like the church-social type, either.

Oh, I knew Dad knew some ladies. He was awarded me for every other vacation. For example, if I spend Christmas vacation with my mother and her husband, then I spend spring vacation with Dad. Then the week between the close of the school year at Ludwell and the opening of Camp Gitcheegoomee I spend with Dad. The week between the closing of Camp Gitcheegoomee and the first day of school I go back to Mother and the doctor. I have what they call equal visitation rights.

What I'm saying is that sometimes Dad forgets that it is his turn for a visit. When I show up some-place, I find that, as hard as it is to get hotel reservations these days, he's been letting some lady use one of the rooms in his suite. It's just logical to think that if he was letting some lady who couldn't get a room of her own use one of his rooms, he would get to know her well enough to have dinner with her, or something like that.

I even met a couple of them. There was a lady in Kansas City who had an allergy to me. Dad explained that was the reason that every time she saw me she would get all red in the face. And there was another blonde lady one time, that was in San Francisco, California, who was using the pool in the hotel to practice for swimming across the entrance to the bay, under the Golden Gate Bridge. She taught me the Australian crawl. I never heard, come to think of it, whether she made it across or not. I suppose she did. I'm sure Dad would have mentioned it if she had drowned. And it probably would have been in the newspapers.

But, as I say, they were just ladies he had met who couldn't get a room, and it never entered my mind that he was thinking of marrying one of them. And now that I thought of it, Miss Amanda Lewis was the first lady he had ever brought to visit me at the Ludwell School. Not that he got a chance to visit me much himself. It's a long drive out here from the airport, and both my mother and father are always saying how impossible the schedule and the connections are. She doesn't get a chance to visit me much, either. She has the twins, my half-sisters, to worry about, and then, too, her husband is a doctor, and everybody knows how overworked they are, and that what they want to do when they get a little time off is just loaf around the pool with their shoes off and not come all the way out here. It's a really nice pool, inside their house, and I know how he feels.

So I really wasn't surprised when a couple of minutes after Miss Amanda Lewis asked me if I wasn't thrilled that she and Dad were going to be married Dad looked at his watch and said they would have to get going if they were going to make their plane.

"But we'll be back, darling," Miss Lewis said to me. "You're going to see a lot more of your daddy from now on."

"I am?" I asked.

"Can I tell him, darling?" Miss Lewis asked my father. "Or would you rather tell him?"

"Just as soon as Amanda and I are married, Rutherford," my father said, "we want you to come to live with us."

"Uh oh," Number Three said. It was really none of his business, and he certainly should have kept his opinions to himself, even if he was my best friend. But what he said out loud was just what I was thinking.

I did manage to find out before they left where he had met her. He was building a dam on the Tennessee River, and after a couple of months of flying down there once a week to see how things were going, he got to know Miss Lewis, who was often on the same plane he was. She worked for the airline. She said she was a passenger comforts coordinator, which is what they call stewardesses on Trans-Tennessee Airways.

Anyway, what happened is that when she had a minute free from coordinating passenger comforts, she confessed to Dad that as long as she had been associated with the aviation industry she had never had a ride in a helicopter. So Dad, being a gentleman and all, offered her a ride on the company helicopter when it met his plane. And one thing apparently led to another.

Number Three knows me well enough to know that I didn't really want to talk about what Miss Amanda Lewis and my father had said about my going to live with them once they got married, so after Dad and Miss Lewis left the subject didn't come up, and I tried not to think about it.

That was kind of hard to do. What I'm saying, as disloyal as this makes me sound, is that I wasn't especially keen to go live with Dad, especially if Miss Amanda Lewis was going to be around. It's not that I don't love my father. But the thing is, I guess I take after my mother. Living in a hotel is all right, I suppose, if you just go there at night to change your clothes and sleep, the way Dad does. But to spend all day in one, day after day, is a very good way to go bananas.

For one thing, it is absolutely impossible to get a good hamburger in a hotel. Generally speaking, they make pretty good club sandwiches; but a good hamburger, much less a good cheeseburger, is something they just don't seem to be able to make. They don't even call them hamburgers. They call them something like "chopped tips of sirloin" or "Salisbury steak." I ordered a cheeseburger one time in a hotel in New Orleans, and you know what I got? I got a hamburger patty the size of a pancake, lying on the plate with two pieces of asparagus laid crosswise on it. I also got a piece of French bread about a foot long, and a little, triangular piece of cheese, white with runny insides, that smelled awful.

For another thing, there is very little to do in a hotel, especially if you're my age. What about the swimming pool and the tennis courts and, sometimes, the paddle-ball courts and the other recreational facilities, you might ask. Well, they're fine. But what most people don't understand is that hotels are operated on the idea that people use them only at night. You try to take a swim at, say, ten o'clock in the morning and what you find is three guys pouring some kind of acid in it and a sign reading POOL CLOSED FOR MAINTENANCE.

The reason you try to take a swim at ten o'clock in the morning is that that's when the chambermaids come to clean up your room. They generally work in pairs, and it's hard to believe how much noise two women can make while changing the sheets and emptying the wastebaskets unless you've lived through it.

So far as tennis and golf are concerned, that doesn't work very often either. For one thing, you can't play tennis by yourself, and it's hard to find a pick-up game on hotel courts. One time I was in Texas with Dad — I forget the name of the hotel — and I did find somebody on the courts who asked me if I wanted to play. We played for a couple of hours. What I didn't know until Dad got the hotel bill and blew his stack was that the guy who asked me if I wanted to knock the ball around was a tennis pro and charged thirty dollars an hour.

You can, of course, play golf by yourself. It's not as much fun as playing with somebody, but it's more fun than sitting around the room watching soap operas. The trouble here is that most hotel golf courses have two signs outside the locker room, before you even get to the first tee. One sign says that use of golf carts is mandatory. The second sign says that the hotel is sorry but children are not permitted to operate golf carts. So far as hotels are concerned, a child is anybody not old enough to drink whiskey in the bar.

What I'm saying is living in a hotel is bad enough by itself; it would really be awful with a stepmother. Especially a stepmother who would probably keep on working as a passenger comforts coordinator. By the time she got home from a hard day at Trans-Tennessee Airways, passing out trays of food that people didn't like very much, I didn't think there would be much of that stewardess-type cheerfulness left over. If you've ever looked at a stewardess when she didn't know you were looking, you know what I mean. They only smile when they know some passenger is looking at them.

Besides, I was pretty used to being at the Ludwell School. After all, I've been here ever since Mother married the doctor. I came here right after the wedding. They dropped me off on the way to their honeymoon. I'll admit I didn't like it at first, but after a while, once I understood how things were run, it was better. To tell you the truth, and I wouldn't want either my father or Junior Ludwell to hear me say this, if I had any choice in the matter, I'd prefer the Ludwell School to living in most any hotel I can think of, and I know a bunch of hotels.

Not that the Ludwell School is perfect. It has its faults. The criminal justice system, for one thing, leaves a lot to be desired. Since Number Three and I got involved with that two days after Dad and Miss Amanda Lewis came up here to pay a visit, I'll tell you about that.

The first thing that happens is the arrest. This takes place at the evening meal, just before Junior Ludwell says grace and we can start to eat. I suppose the whole idea of doing it then is to start the punishment by making the criminals lose their appetites. What happens is that Junior Ludwell stands up at the head table and coughs. Sometimes this works, and sometimes it doesn't. Most of the time, actually, he has to bang on one of the stainless-steel water pitchers with his knife to get our attention.

"Young gentlemen," Junior Ludwell began on the evening in question, "there are a few announcements." The few announcements he was talking about took only about a minute to announce. Not very much happens at the Ludwell School on Tuesdays. I think the announcements he made that night had something to do with the showing in the auditorium of a Hopalong Cassidy movie, for those who were not on either academic or disciplinary restriction.

Academic restriction means, generally, that you've flunked a test or that some master has turned you in for not doing your homework. Until you pass the test or come up with the homework, you're not allowed to watch Hopalong Cassidy movies in the auditorium, for example. So far, nobody seems to have told Junior Ludwell that the local television station shows Hopalong Cassidy movies all the time, or that they are now making television sets small enough to hide in dresser drawers.

Not keeping up with your schoolwork at Ludwell is a lot harder than it sounds. The minute you start to fall behind, Ludwell has what they call supervised

study. This means that instead of doing your homework in your room you do it in the library, under
the eyes of a live-in guard. If you have trouble, you
are supposed to ask the assistance of the guard. It
is not normally necessary to ask for assistance. The
live-in guards practically stand over your shoulder.
If there were no inmates doing supervised study, the
live-in guards wouldn't have to be in the library,
either. The sooner an inmate catches up with his
studies, the sooner the live-in guards can get back
to pulling the wings off flies, or whatever they do
for fun on their off time.

Disciplinary restriction is something else. Persons
on disciplinary restriction, called Hardened Criminals (as opposed to ordinary inmates) have been
caught doing something wrong or against the rules.
Hardened criminals are punished in several ways,
depending on the offense, but all of them are made
an example of.

Right in front of the head table are two tables set
aside for hardened criminals. The food is the same,
but you have to go get it yourself instead of having
it served by a student waiter. There is no tablecloth,
no little vase with a flower in it, and no condiments
like ketchup, steak sauce, or Tabasco. And hardened
criminals are forbidden to talk to each other while
eating. But aside from the no Tabasco, sometimes
being at the hardened criminals' tables is a relief,

especially if the live-in guards normally make you eat with the animals, as some of us refer to our football, baseball, and soccer players.

After he had made the day's announcements, Ludwell Junior looked sad and got down to the business at hand. "I am very sorry, young gentlemen," he said, "to be forced to tell you that within our student body we have at least one and *very possibly two* individuals who have committed a very serious act of vandalism in the Thomas Cushman Memorial Administrative Annex."

Thomas Cushman was another alumnus. When he died, he left the school money to buy some electric typewriters and filing cabinets for the office, so they named the office the Thomas Cushman Memorial Administrative Annex.

Ludwell Junior's announcement really got everybody's attention. A very serious act of vandalism could mean almost anything. For a moment, especially when Number Three looked at me and shrugged his shoulders, I thought that maybe he was talking about something else.

"Some person, or *persons*, unknown," Ludwell Junior went on, "for reasons I *cannot* imagine, surreptitiously entered the Thomas Cushman Memorial Administrative Annex on Visitor's Day, when our beloved administrator, Miss Eunice Wattlebury, was momentarily absent. And then this person, or *per-*

sons, using what we believe to be a substance known as Ajax One-Drop-Holds-a-Ton Miracle Glue, glued every other drawer in Miss Wattlebury's Daily Student Record file cabinet shut."

He was talking about us, all right.

Chapter 3

Junior Ludwell paused to let this sink in. I wondered how he knew it was Ajax One-Drop-Holds-a-Ton Miracle Glue. I looked over at Number Three. He was making a face, as if he had just thought of something unpleasant. The perfect crime we had so carefully plotted and executed had obviously been solved.

What had happened was this: Number Three and I had been in the Thomas Cushman Memorial Administrative Annex emptying wastebaskets when we saw how the Daily Student Record system worked. Or how, so to speak, the system could be kept from working.

It was a negative-comment-only system. In other words, the only time they put something about you in the file was when you had done something wrong. One of the masters, or maybe the coach, or the nurse, or Junior Ludwell himself, would catch an inmate doing something wrong or not doing something he was supposed to be doing. The warden was then supposed to write down the nature of the offense on a little piece of paper made up specifically for that purpose. And then the next time he or she was in the office, the warden was supposed to empty his pocket or her purse of the little piece of paper and transfer the report of the crime to the individual student's card in the Daily Student Record filing cabinet. Then, once a day, Ludwell Junior would come into the Administrative Annex and check to see what crimes had been committed. He would take the cards of criminals with him.

What happened was that we saw Senora Gabriella Dumos-Santos, who teaches music appreciation and piano and is faculty adviser to the Ludwell School A Cappella Choir, come into the administrative annex with a couple of crime reports in her purse. She went to the filing cabinet, pulled out the drawer holding the file card of one of the inmates, and transferred the details of his crime to his card. Then she started to do the same thing for another criminal, but the file drawer with his card in it was stuck. She jerked on it, but it still wouldn't open, which meant that it was really stuck, because Senora Dumos-Santos is what you might call a sturdy lady. If a stuck drawer she yanked on stayed stuck, it was really stuck.

So what Senora Dumos-Santos did, after saying something in Spanish about broken fingernails, was to lay the crime report on top of the filing cabinet. That made sense. Ludwell Junior would see it when he went to the cabinet.

What happened, though, was that no more than two minutes after Senora Dumos-Santos had put the crime report slip on top of the filing cabinet where Ludwell Junior would see it, Miss Wattlebury walked past the filing cabinet and saw it.

Miss Wattlebury is what you could call compulsively neat. A place for everything and everything in its place. The place for little slips of paper, so far as Miss Wattlebury is concerned, is in the wastebasket, and that's where the crime report slip she found on top of the filing cabinet went.

That criminal, thanks to a stuck drawer, was to go scot free.

The thing to do was to make sure the drawers in which our cards were filed somehow got stuck. But we didn't just leap into that. We thought it through. If we glued shut only the drawers with our names on them, that was certain to cause suspicion. So what we finally did, when we got around to taking the necessary action, was to glue shut half of the drawers.

We figured that with a little bit of luck, it would take two, maybe three weeks before it occurred to Miss Wattlebury that she should report the stuck-drawer problem to Mr. Birdwell, the janitor, and probably two weeks after that before Mr. Birdwell actually got around to unsticking them. For as long as that took, we were home free.

"I hardly need tell you," Ludwell Junior went on, "that Mr. Birdwell, our hard-working chief of maintenance, has far more important things to do with his time than spend most of the day unsticking file drawers. And if Mr. Birdwell hadn't known, as one more asset in his fund of professional knowledge, so to speak, that Ajax One-Ton-Holds-a-Drop . . . One-*Drop*-Holds-a-*Ton* Miracle Glue can be released by the use of nail-polish remover, there's simply no telling how much damage would have been done to the file drawers. As it was, Mr. Birdwell had to spend all morning and most of the afternoon dripping nail-polish remover into the cracks with an eye dropper."

There was another pause, during which Ludwell Junior swept the room with his eyes, looking into the eyes of everybody in it. He's really pretty good at this. When I first came to Ludwell and he looked in my eyes like this, I was willing to confess to doing whatever he was sore about then, even if I didn't know what it was. But by now, of course, I'm pretty used to it. When he looks at me now, I just cross my eyes.

"A very detailed, *very* thorough investigation has been under way," he went on, "ever since Miss Wattlebury came to me — and she was very upset — to report this outrage. The investigation is nearly complete. I should like to take this opportunity to remind the person, or *persons*, guilty of this outrage that things will go easier on him, or *them*, if they come forward at this time and make a clean breast of it."

His eyes swept the room again. They met mine again. I crossed mine again.

"Let us pray," Ludwell Junior said.

There was still a very good chance that he was bluffing. But several things worried me. For one thing, he knew it was Ajax One-Drop-Holds-a-Ton Miracle Glue. For another, he seemed to suspect that more than one person was involved. And, more important, Number Three looked sick. More than anyone else, Number Three should have known whether Junior Ludwell was bluffing. Junior was, after all, his father.

There was no way I could talk it over with Number Three at supper. We are considered a disruptive influence on each other and on the dining hall in general and they make us eat at separate tables. But we met afterward, by the garbage cans outside the dining-hall kitchen.

That's where The Thing eats his supper. Mr. Abraham Lincoln O'Malley, our executive chef, got tired of having The Thing sneak into the kitchen to help himself, so he got another garbage can and had "The Thing" painted on it and put it next to the can with "Edible Garbage" painted on it. It's our job to stand there and watch The Thing eat, and then put whatever he doesn't want in with the rest of the edible garbage.

The main reason we have to do that is that when The Thing is eating, he won't let anybody except us within fifty feet of him. One time when he was working on a large bone, The Thing kept the kitchen staff in the kitchen until half-past seven, and they filed a complaint, and since that Number Three and I have had to come and watch him eat.

"I guess," Number Three said, wincing a little at the noise The Thing was making crunching bones, "that I'd better go over to the House and confess. Get it over with."

"I think he's bluffing," I said. "He may suspect us, but I don't think anyone saw us go in or come out of the office."

"He may suspect you," Number Three said, "but he knows about me."

"How can he know about you?"

"You know the little pieces of cardboard the Ajax One-Drop-Holds-a-Ton Miracle Glue came in?"

"They call them blister pack cards," I said. "What about them?"

"Well, I was careful to put them in my back pocket after I took the glue tubes out. I didn't want to leave them lying around the annex. They probably had our fingerprints on them."

"Good thinking, Number Three."

"But then, after your father and his stewardess were in the cell, I forgot about them."

"How do you mean forgot about them?"

"I left them in my pants. When I took them home to be washed, I mean. I think that's the very detailed investigation my father was talking about. My mother found the whatdidyoucallthem, the blister cards, when she washed my pants."

"That was pretty stupid of you, Number Three," I said.

"Yeah," he agreed. "But since it was my fault, I'll take the rap. I'll say it was all my idea and that I did it all by myself."

Well, of course I couldn't let him do that, even if what he had done was that stupid. So the next morning Number Three and I found ourselves in phase two of the Ludwell School criminal justice procedure. This consists of either being found guilty or, in our case, confessing. Then comes the lecture, and finally, the announcement of punishment.

To cut a long and painful story short, and to pass

over a very long lecture, I'll get right to the punishment part. Normally, when a serious crime is committed, the criminals get the worst punishment Junior Ludwell can think of. This is denial of home-visit privilege. This means that the next long weekend (or the next two or three long weekends, depending on the seriousness of the crime), when you could go home, you don't get to go.

In our case, of course, this wouldn't work. Not only was Number Three's home right there on the campus, but there was no way Junior Ludwell was going to keep his mate from having Ludwell Three for Sunday dinner at home, no matter what he had done. He could have burned down the Thomas Cushman Memorial Administrative Annex, not just glued a couple of file drawers shut, and he still would have had dinner with his mother. She was still pretty sore at Junior Ludwell for making Number Three live in Foxcroft Hall, and Junior was not about to make her any madder by telling her Number Three couldn't come home for Sunday dinner. And as for me, with the absolutely impossible airline schedules and the doctor all worn out after a hard week at the plastic-surgery clinic and my father generally out of the country on home-visit weekends, I never got to take advantage of home-visit weekends anyway.

Another standard punishment was getting thrown out of your room. So far as most inmates were concerned, some cells were more desirable than other cells. Some guys wanted to live on the ground floor, and some guys wanted to live in rooms by themselves. Rooms were assigned on the basis of seniority. Seniority depended on good behavior. If you lost your seniority, some other guy could claim your room. The whole idea was that the saints of Foxcroft Hall would occupy the good rooms, and the sinners, in order, the less desirable rooms, with the all-around champion sinners stuck up in the attic. Since Number Three and I already lived in the attic, that particular punishment was out of the game.

One time about a year ago, when Frog-Eyes (on his birth certificate it says Bartholomew) Davis, the nearest thing we've got to a football hero, was really in trouble, Junior Ludwell tried to move him into the attic as punishment. What Frog-Eyes had got caught doing was smuggling a six-pack of beer off the school bus when the football team went to a social evening and hymn sing at a church in town, which was run by the same reverend who backed into the lake when The Thing growled at him. Frog-Eyes was really in trouble because both Junior Ludwell and the reverend were still pretty touchy about what the reverend had said about a school where the chapel was named after a man who had made his mark in the world as a sour-mash whiskey distiller.

Junior Ludwell told Frog-Eyes that his thoughtless,

not to say forbidden, act of taking intoxicants to a church run by a teetotaling reverend had brought disgrace upon the good name of the Ludwell School. Frog-Eyes was ordered to move out of his second-floor-front single room with bath and up into the attic with us. That was supposed to teach him something about the humiliation Junior Ludwell had felt when the reverend had clapped Frog-Eyes in a friendly way on the back and two bottles of beer had fallen out of his Ludwell Lions zipper jacket and smashed on the sidewalk in front of the reverend's church.

What really humiliated Frog-Eyes was *The Thing*. Like a lot of football players I have known, Frog-Eyes talks a lot. One of the things he talked a lot about was how he wasn't afraid of The Thing. It was just a dog, Frog-Eyes said, and the only reason The Thing got away with what he did was because he sensed that people were afraid of him. *He* never had any trouble with The Thing, Frog-Eyes said, because The Thing knew *he* wasn't afraid of him.

Junior Ludwell had told Frog-Eyes what his punishment was the same way he told everybody: that is, first thing in the morning after breakfast and before class. He told Frog-Eyes to move his clothes and stuff out of his second-floor-front single room and up into the attic and then go to class.

Well, Frog-Eyes never showed up in class, and

when some of the live-in guards went looking for him, they couldn't find him. So a search party, including all the inmates, was formed. Number Three told me later that what his father was really worried about was that Frog-Eyes would be so humiliated by having to move in with us that he would run away. Running away from the Ludwell School, because of the disgrace it brings to the good name of the school, is really a high crime, like treason.

Einstein Feinberg was the one who found Frog-Eyes. While everybody else was looking in closets and places like that, Einstein Feinberg went at it intellectually. He assembled all the facts and examined them critically. He put himself in Frog-Eyes's shoes. He thought there was something strange about the way The Thing was just sitting in the cell, looking out the window instead of running around helping us find Frog-Eyes. So he put his head out the window and looked around, and there was Frog-Eyes, sitting on the top of the roof, both arms wrapped around a chimney.

As a result of all that, Junior Ludwell pardoned Frog-Eyes. He understood that it was really enough humiliation for Frog-Eyes to have himself chased out a window by a dog, when he had been telling everybody he wasn't afraid of that particular dog. And even more humiliating for a football star to have the fire department have to come out from town to get him off the roof. On the way up, with The Thing after him, he had temporarily forgotten that he was afraid of heights, but once he had got up on top of the roof and it was pretty clear that The Thing was too smart to go out there himself, Frog-Eyes remembered it all again.

As I was saying, finding a punishment to fit our crime posed something of a problem to Junior Ludwell. He really had to give it quite a bit of thought. When he finally figured out what it was, it was half good and half bad.

We got the usual two weeks in solitary confinement, of course. That meant we had to sit at the hardened criminals' tables (one of us at each table) in the dining hall, and our privilege to watch Hopalong Cassidy movies in the auditorium was withdrawn. And, for the next two weeks, in place of what the catalogue calls supervised recreation between the last class and supper, we had to go work for Miss Wattlebury in the Thomas Cushman Memorial Administrative Annex.

That isn't really as bad as it sounds. What Junior Ludwell had in mind was that Miss Wattlebury would have us put records back where they belong in the filing cabinets, or polish the furniture, or something like that. But as long as we've been around the Ludwell School, we've had time to figure Miss Wattlebury out. She doesn't want us putting records back in the filing cabinets where they belong. She says it's a mystery to her how anybody as old as we are could be so dumb as to file things that should go under *B* under *G* or *X*, and her bottom line is that it's more trouble for her to have us put records and stuff back where they belong than it is to do it herself.

So far as washing the windows is concerned, or polishing the furniture, the way to get around that is simply to ask Miss Wattlebury a question. For example, "Miss Wattlebury, what's an aardvark?" Thirty seconds after you ask her a question like that, she's got you sitting down at a table with a pencil and pad to take notes, and she's running over to the library to bring you everything from the *Encyclopedia Brittanica* to twenty-five-year-old copies of *National Geographic* magazine, everything in the library that even mentions the aardvark, and she has completely forgotten about getting her windows washed or the furniture polished. There's a lot of interesting stuff in the encyclopedia if you find yourself with the time to sit down and read one.

What Junior Ludwell came up with that really was punishment was an assignment to write a 3500-word essay on why people should respect Ludwell School property and not go around gluing file drawers closed.

Now, there are some people for whom that sort of assignment wouldn't pose any problems. Einstein

Feinberg, for one. Intellectual and cultural endeavors like that are right down Einstein's alley. Or Slinky Martinson, who says he's already writing an epic poem, whatever that is. But for someone like myself, who wants to become a construction engineer like my father, writing thirty-five words, all spelled right, much less 3500, is really cruel and unusual punishment and is probably illegal anywhere but at the Ludwell School.

Chapter 4

I remember the first day Moose Hanrahan came to school for a number of reasons. For one thing, Grandfather called me up. Inmates are not supposed to get telephone calls except between five-thirty and lights out, unless in case of emergency. Inmates in solitary confinement aren't supposed to get them at all. Parents and/or guardians calling up expecting to talk to their inmate find themselves talking instead to one of the live-in guards, or maybe to Junior Ludwell himself, about what rule the inmate has broken and how he is progressing through the supervised correctional instruction, which is what they call solitary confinement.

Grandfather called me about half-past ten in the morning, which is about the time they wake him up in the Athletic Club, where he lives. My father says that the Athletic Club is so much like a hotel that Grandfather has no right to make cracks about his living in hotels. Grandfather says that when Grandmother was alive, they lived in houses for thirty-six years, raising their son, which is thirty-six more years than my father ever lived in any house raising his, and furthermore, anyone seventy-seven years old can live anyplace he pleases.

I get to stay in the Athletic Club every once in a while, when a home-visit weekend coincides with a room's being open, and I like it. We have to keep this sort of a secret from my mother. For some reason she's got it in for the Athletic Club. My father says this is because she went there one time looking for him. It was during the time they were getting divorced, and my father was living there. She didn't believe the steward when he told her he didn't think my father was there, and she didn't pay any attention to the steward when he told her he didn't think she should go looking for him in the pool. She was pretty sure my father was back there and just didn't want to see her at that moment. So she went to find out for herself. She was right. My father was there all right, sitting at a table by the side of the swimming pool, drinking beer. There were a bunch of other members there, too, either drinking beer or swimming around in the pool. What my mother didn't know was that, to save on laundry costs I guess, and because the pool is off limits to females, you don't wear bathing suits in the pool.

After Mother walked in like that and found my father and grandfather and all the other members in their birthday suits, she decided that the Athletic Club was and is, as she says the minute anybody even mentions the name, a collection of dirty old men sitting around getting drunk in the nude. When the divorce went through, Mother was still so mad about it that she tried to have it written into the custody agreement that my father was forbidden to take me to the Athletic Club. As it happened, the judge belonged to the Athletic Club and didn't much like being called a dirty old man, so that part of the custody agreement got crossed off.

I am *legally* allowed to go there, but we try, without coming right out and lying about it, to keep my mother from finding out when I do. If you've ever had any experience with a woman with a temper, you understand the problem. The last time she found out about it she called my father in Phoenix, Arizona — collect — and spent thirty minutes telling him what she thought about my being there.

Well, anyway, about the time they normally wake Grandfather up at the Athletic Club and bring him what he calls his eye-opener, which is when I was in English III, "Shakespeare's Sonnets," I was called out of class and handed the telephone.

"Is that you, Runt?" he asked.

"Yes, sir. Is anything wrong, Grandfather?"

"I really hope not," he said. "Tell me, Runt, you still got the *Bubo virginianus?*"

"Yes, sir. I brushed his feathers just like you told me to, last night."

"I don't suppose you've seen your father or heard from him lately, have you?"

"As a matter of fact, Grandfather, he was up here weekend before last."

"You weren't sick or anything, were you, Runt? I distinctly told that dummy who runs that place I was to be informed the moment you so much as sneezed."

"No, sir, I wasn't sick," I said.

"You mean your father went up there just to pay you a visit?"

"Yes, sir."

"Now, Runt, I want you to understand I have my reasons for asking, and that I certainly don't want to sound like your mother, but did it look like your father was drinking?"

"No, sir," I said. "What's this all about, Grandfather?"

"I don't want you to get worried, Runt, but some

very disturbing rumors about your father are crawling around the construction-business grapevine."

"What kind of disturbing rumors?" I asked.

He didn't answer me. He asked another question. "He didn't happen to mention, did he, that he'd made any new friends lately? Lady friends?"

"He had one with him," I said.

"He did, did he? Now tell me this, Runt: You've seen enough of them to be able to spot one, even in civilian clothes. Did this one look like an airline stewardess?"

"Yes, sir," I said. "But she's not a stewardess. She corrected me when I called her that. She's a passenger comforts coordinator."

"And did your father seem, what shall I say, *fond* of this passenger comforter?"

"He said he's going to marry her," I said.

"My God, it's worse than I thought!"

"And she says that as soon as they get married and buy a house, I'm going to go live with them."

"Over my dead body," Grandfather said. "I'd rather see you living with your hot-tempered mother and her face-lift specialist. But don't you worry about a thing, Runt. Trust your grandfather. And when you give my regards to Mr. Lushwell, tell him the emergency is over and not to worry."

"That's Ludwell, Grandfather," I corrected him. "And what emergency?"

"He said he couldn't let me talk to you unless it was an emergency, so I told him of course it was an emergency. Now you tell him it's over. Behave yourself, Runt. Your poor old grandfather has got enough on his tired old shoulders worrying about your father and his stewardess without your getting in any more trouble."

"Yes, sir."

The second reason I remember the first day Moose Hanrahan came to the Ludwell School is that that was the day I thought I got a letter from my father, except that it turned out to be a letter from Miss Amanda Lewis. The reason I thought it was a letter from my father is that it came in a construction-company envelope and was postmarked Key Biscayne, Florida. The only people I knew who would be mailing me something in a company envelope from Key Biscayne, Florida, were Grandfather and my father, and I already knew that it wasn't from Grandfather, so I thought it had to be from my father.

It wasn't. It was from Miss Amanda Lewis.

"Dearest Rutherford," she wrote. She wrote sort of funny. Instead of dots over the *i*'s, she used little circles. She also used purple ink. It looked something like those menus you get in fancy French restaurants, except that you could read her writing, and you usually have to guess at what it says on the menus in French restaurants, the writing being so awful. It was also the first time anybody had ever called me Dearest Rutherford.

What she wrote was: "Just a line to let you know that your daddy and I are looking very hard for a suitable house for us all to live in after we're married. And I think I've found just the place. I think it's just *darling*, and the real-estate man, who has been very helpful, has told me in confidence that it's a real bargain and that we'd almost be stealing it. I am enclosing a Polaroid photograph of it. I think it would help your father to make up his mind if you wrote him a letter and told him you'd like to live in it. There's a *darling* little apartment over the garage you could have. Be sure to write and tell him you would like to live in it."

When I looked at the picture, the first thing I thought was that she had put the wrong one in the envelope. The house looked like a cross between one of your larger funeral homes and a Howard Johnson's Restaurant. The reason I mention Howard Johnson's is that I have never seen a funeral home with a bright orange tile roof. Aside from that, the house looked more like a funeral home, mainly because the garage she was talking about was certainly big enough to take care of all the hearses and limousines even a very successful funeral home could ever want. Miss Amanda Lewis had drawn two little arrows on the picture. One of them pointed to the funeral home and said "Daddy & Me!" The other one pointed to the garage and said "You!" She was apparently pretty excited about the funeral home.

To tell you the truth, I wasn't exactly thrilled at the idea of going to live over a garage behind a funeral home in Florida. When I showed the picture to Number Three, he didn't make things any better. He said the house reminded him of a movie about the French Revolution he had once seen. Number Three said the hero of the movie, a duke or something like that, had lived in a house like the one in the picture until the revolutionaries had come to carry him off in a little wagon to the guillotine.

Well, it wasn't hard to make up my mind what to do. I wasn't about to lie to my father, but on the other hand, I didn't want to hurt Miss Amanda Lewis's feelings, since she had been good enough to ask my opinion. I decided the best thing to do was pretend I never got the letter and the picture.

That was the day Moose Hanrahan came to the orphanage.

Whenever a new inmate joins the orphanage, there is a little traditional ceremony. It takes place at supper. The way the dining hall is set up, the live-in guards, also known as the faculty, sit on one side of a long table against the wall. The inmates sit at maybe three dozen smaller tables, six inmates to a table. Right up in front, between the inmate tables and the faculty table, are the two tables where the hardened criminals eat. Number Three and I were sitting there, of course, as a result of the glued-shut filing-cabinet drawers in the Thomas Cushman Memorial Administrative Annex. Number Three was at one table and I was at the other one. There were also a couple of guys on academic restriction at each table.

The tables for the hardened criminals are the tables closest to the faculty table for two reasons: It's easier for the live-in guards to make sure the hardened criminals don't talk while they are supposed to be thinking about their crimes; and, Junior thinks it places the criminals in a position of shame, where the rest of the inmates can see them.

Whenever there is a new inmate, he gets to sit at the faculty table for his first supper. He gets to sit right next to Junior Ludwell in the seat where Junior's mate, otherwise known as Mrs. Ludwell, usually sits.

On this evening, after everybody had finished supper the welcome ceremony began. Junior Ludwell stood up and smiled. This was the signal for the dozen or so inmates Ludwell calls junior counselors and we call trustees to start making hissing noises.

This was supposed to call the attention of the others to the fact that Junior was about to make a special announcement, and that we should all, as young gentlemen, start paying attention.

It seldom works, after supper any better than before supper, and it didn't work that night either. Before he got the other inmates to stop talking, Junior Ludwell had to bang on the stainless-steel water pitcher with his knife handle. But finally there was silence.

"Young gentlemen," Junior Ludwell announced. "We have a new member of the Ludwell family." By that, he didn't mean that he and his mate had just presented Number Three with a new baby brother or sister. He meant there was a new inmate.

"I would like to introduce J. Monroe Hanrahan," Junior Ludwell said. "Stand up, Monroe."

J. Monroe Hanrahan stood up. He was so large that, for a moment, I thought there were two of him. Normally, Junior would show what a friendly guy he was by putting his arm around the new inmate's shoulders. There was no way he could do this with J. Monroe Hanrahan. Junior's arm wouldn't reach up that far. And when he led J. Monroe Hanrahan out from behind the faculty table for the next part of the ceremony, it looked just like one of those nature-in-the-wild films on television. The moose walking slowly along after the baby moose. The fat little baby moose bouncing along as fast as it can go, and the moose having a hard time going that slowly.

"And how do we welcome a newcomer?" Junior Ludwell said, when the two of them were standing in front of the faculty table.

One of the junior counselors jumped to his feet and signaled for the rest of us to stand up. Moose Hanrahan looked as if he might be sick to his stomach.

"One, two, three, four," the junior counselor began. "For he's a jolly good fellow, for he's a jolly good fellow . . ."

After the junior counselor had maybe half of the inmates singing somewhat louder than a whisper, he turned with a smile to get the newcomer's reaction.

At that moment I knew I would have to get to know this new inmate a lot better. He was my kind of guy. Apparently not caring whether Junior Ludwell saw him or not, he gave the choir leader the finger.

Number Three immediately started to applaud. I joined in, and so did most of the others. Junior was delighted. He turned around, looked up at Moose Hanrahan, and beamed. By that time, of course, Moose had stopped giving the choir leader the finger. He wore a smile himself, a self-satisfied smile.

"Well, fellas," Junior said, when the singing was

over, "that certainly was a fine welcome to Monroe, and I'm sure he's grateful to you all."

More applause. Moose nodded his head.

"You may all be excused," Junior Ludwell said, "except for Mr. Peters and Mr. Ludwell. I would like to have a word with them."

I wondered what that was all about. Our two weeks as hardened criminals still had three days to go. It wasn't time for the friendly little talk that always came when your sentence was up. And I was no further than 200 words into my 3500-word essay on why you shouldn't glue card-catalogue drawers shut.

We walked up to where Junior stood with Moose Hanrahan and waited until the others had left the dining room.

"Monroe," Junior said. "I would like you to meet Rutherford Peters II and James Foxcroft Ludwell III."

"Call me Moose," J. Monroe Hanrahan said.

"We . . . uh . . . try not to use *unflattering* nicknames at the Ludwell School," Junior said. "Wouldn't you rather have the fellows call you Monroe?"

"No," Moose said flatly. "I'd rather have them call me Moose. You got something against mooses?"

"Not at all," Junior said quickly. "Well, Monroe," he went on, "what I have decided to do is put you in the hands of these two fellows."

"What for?" Moose inquired.

"Well, they can show you the ropes — teach you something of our ways, and the traditions of the school, our system of rewards and, I'm afraid, punishments."

"Okay," Moose said. "Why not?"

"And in appreciation for the warm way you welcomed Monroe to our school," Junior said to us, "because I saw how nicely both of you applauded when we were singing 'For He's a Jolly Good Fellow,' and for taking Monroe in hand, you may consider the balance of your disciplinary period suspended. You may rejoin the others as of breakfast."

"Gee, Pop, do I have to?" Number Three asked.

"James, you know that I do not appreciate being referred to as Pop," Junior said. "And we'll have no more of your odd sense of humor." He turned to Moose. "And you, Monroe: I hope that being associated with Rutherford and James will make you reconsider your decision."

Moose didn't reply.

"Rutherford and James will help you carry your things from the office to the room," Junior said. "Good evening, gentlemen."

"Good evening," Number Three and I said in unison.

"See you around," Moose said. He looked at me. "Rutherford? *Rutherford?* It sounds like some town in New Jersey."

"Call me Pete," I said.

"I hope your father isn't going to hold his breath," he said to Number Three, "until I change my decision."

"What decision is that, Moose?" Number Three asked.

"I'm not going to play football," Moose said. "Period."

"Oh!" I said. "That explains a lot."

"A lot of what?" Moose asked.

"Why he put you with us," I said.

"Why did he?"

"We don't play football either," Number Three said.

"No fooling? Why not?" Moose said. His face lit up with interest.

"I figured it out when I was ten," Number Three said. "When you play football, people walk on your face a lot. Particularly if you're small."

"Small, huh? You ought to try it big," Moose said. "The bigger you are, the more of you there is to knock down and jump on."

I had never considered that before, but there was obviously something to it.

"Around here, though," Number Three said, "if you don't play football, there are problems."

Chapter 5

"What kind of problems?" Moose inquired. Number Three had turned him around and pointed him toward the office so we could get his things.

"D.O.D. is a football freak," Number Three said.

"D.O.D?"

"Dear Old Dad," Number Three explained. "He played football when he was here, and when he was in college, and he's all for it."

"That figures," Moose said. "He's a fat little guy. It probably doesn't hurt fat little guys as much when they get stepped on."

"Whatever," Number Three said. "But the point

is, if you don't play football around here, you're considered unpatriotic."

"So what does that mean?"

"It means you get to cut a lot of grass during football season," I said. "When the other guys are practicing, and when they're away playing, if you don't play football, you cut grass."

"What's that got to do with it?" Moose asked. We were now outside the Thomas Cushman Memorial Administrative Annex. There were a footlocker and three suitcases by the door. Moose picked up the footlocker with one hand, the largest suitcase with the other. Number Three grabbed the smaller of the other two suitcases before I could get to it, so I had to pick up the other one. We started across the campus to the residence hall.

"I asked, what has cutting grass got to do with not playing football?" Moose repeated.

"Aside from the opportunity it gives you to step on other people's faces," Number Three said, "what are the benefits of football?"

"Beats me." Moose shrugged his shoulders.

"It provides healthy exercise in the healthy outdoors," I said. "And so do cutting grass and raking leaves."

"Raking leaves?"

"After the grass stops growing," Number Three said, "you rake leaves. And when the leaves stop falling and it starts to snow, you shovel snow. Right now, I would say we are just about through cutting grass and about to start raking leaves."

"Still beats football," Moose said. By now, with Number Three and me almost out of breath keeping up with him, we were at the residence hall. "Tell me about the driving training program," Moose said.

"The driving program?" Number Three asked. I could tell that he wanted to laugh but wasn't sure that would be wise under the circumstances.

"Yeah, the driving program," Moose said. "That was the main reason I agreed to come here."

That was too much for me. I started to giggle. Moose put down the footlocker he had in his left hand and picked me up, suitcase and all.

"Look, Runt," he said. "When I ask a question, it's not nice to laugh at me." I wondered how he had learned my name.

"If the driving training program is why you came to Ludwell, Moose," Number Three said, "I'm afraid you're going to be disappointed."

"I asked him," Moose said. He held me a little higher in the air, as if to make sure Number Three knew whom he meant.

"The thing is, Moose," I said, "the driving training program isn't what you might think it is from reading the Ludwell School catalogue."

"It isn't?" he asked.

"If you'll just put me down," I said, "I'll be happy to tell you all about it."

"All right," he said, reasonably. "Don't laugh at me anymore and we'll get along fine."

"Right," I said. "Would you rather wait till we get to our room, or would you like me to tell you right here?"

"Right here," Moose said.

"Well, you must have seen the picture in the catalogue that shows one of the inmates and one of the guards standing by a school station wagon. The one where it says, 'Among other extracurricular activities, the Ludwell School offers driving training'?"

"That's what I mean," Moose replied. "What about it?"

"The cold truth is," I said, "that the only way the inmates get anywhere near a school station wagon is when one of the guards takes them into town to see the dentist, or something like that."

"You mean the catalogue lies?" Moose asked.

"Not exactly," I said. "We do have some go-carts."

His face lit up. "Those little teensy cars?" he asked. "*Voom voom voom?*"

"Right," I said. "And there's a quarter-of-a-mile track. When the track-and-field freaks aren't using it, you can take one of the go-carts and go around and around in circles. That's the driving training program."

"Gee," Moose replied, as if a great weight had been lifted off his shoulders. "For a minute there I was afraid you were going to tell me there wasn't a driving training program, or that there was something wrong with it."

"The idea of going around and around a cinder track in a go-cart, going *voom voom voom*, appeals to you?" Number Three asked.

"Yeah," Moose said. "That sounds like fun."

"Where did you say you were from, Moose?" I asked.

"New York City," Moose said. "You have to be eighteen years old to get a license there. So I figured if I came here, I could get lots of practice before I'm ready for my driver's test."

"Well, Moose," Number Three said, "you won't have that problem here. You don't even need a learner's permit to drive one of our go-carts."

"Okay," Moose said. "When can I start?"

"Soon," I said. "Soon."

"Hey, big fella!" a voice called. A couple of the ball freaks came around the side of the house. You know the type. They always have to have some sort of a ball to keep their hands busy. A baseball in baseball season. A basketball in basketball season. And now, in football season, a football.

It wasn't hard to tell why they were smiling. One look at Moose was all they needed to decide that he was just what the Ludwell Lions needed.

"If you're talking to me," Moose said, "don't call me 'big fella'! I don't like it."

"Want to toss the ball around before it gets dark?" one of the ball freaks asked.

"No," Moose said.

Either the ball freak didn't hear him or he ignored him, for the ball came spinning over. I thought for a moment it was going to hit Moose right in the nose. The possibilities of that were interesting to think about. But at the last second, as if he were swatting a fly, Moose put out one of his huge hands and grabbed the ball. In his hand the football looked like a toy.

Moose looked at it as if it were a strange object, the likes of which he had never seen before and didn't much admire now that he had.

"I told you, no," he said, and tossed the ball back, underhanded.

"Not like that," the ball freak said. "Put some zip in it! Like this!"

He snapped the ball back in a spiral. I have noticed that about ball freaks. They work off their excess energy by throwing balls just as hard as they can. Nothing makes them happier than when they can sprain the other guy's thumb, except when they hit him in the stomach with a real zinger.

This one came at Moose just as hard as the ball freak could throw it, aimed right at his stomach. Even Moose seemed to sense that the ball freak had something in mind besides throwing him the ball. He put up both hands to catch the ball. When it hit, there was a sharp crack.

"I already told you I don't want to play," Moose said. "You weren't listening to me."

He grabbed the ball in his right hand, cocked his hand behind his head, and threw. He didn't throw the ball back to the ball freak. He threw it over the residence hall, which is three floors plus a steep roof high. The ball looked like an antiaircraft rocket.

The ball freak and his pals, who had been facing in our direction, turned around to look at the ball. Their eyes got big and their mouths sagged open as the ball disappeared over the roof. There was a moment's silence, and then there came, faintly but very clearly, the tinkling sound of breaking glass. A lot of breaking glass. As if the football had gone through a large window. A very large window.

Headmaster's House, which was a block away, had a glassed-in front porch. It was glassed in with large sheets of plate glass. Number Three had told me how he hated to sit on the front porch with his parents. He said it made him feel like a dummy in a department-store window.

And all at once everybody remembered — even the ball freaks, who weren't known for having very good memories — that Junior Ludwell and his mate were in the habit of sitting on their glassed-in front porch after they went home after supper.

The ball freaks took off at a dead run down the street toward the library.

"Come on, Moose," I said, picking up one of his suitcases. Number Three grabbed the other one, and we ran into the residence hall. Moose picked up the footlocker and the other suitcase and walked slowly after us.

For the first time I remembered The Thing. We had forgotten about him. The Thing was now having his supper out of his private garbage can behind the dining hall, and here we were going up to the cell with Moose. If we didn't show up to watch him eat, The Thing would get worried and come looking for us. The first place he would look, of course, would be in our cell. And if there was one thing The Thing didn't like, it was being surprised. When he saw Moose in the cell, he would really be surprised. I remembered what had happened when The Thing had been surprised to find Frog-Eyes Davis in our cell.

To tell you the truth, you could say that what I decided to do about it wasn't exactly honorable. I was still a little sore about the way Moose had picked me up like that to ask a question. I decided that it would probably be a very good idea for Moose to learn that Number Three and I had a 125-pound furry friend who liked to chew on people. I wasn't going to go as far as letting The Thing actually take a chunk out of Moose, of course. After he had had a chance to show Moose his teeth, and maybe growl at him a little, I would pick up my stuffed owl and wave it around and The Thing would stop growling and showing his teeth and hide under my bed.

By the time Number Three and I had carried Moose's suitcases up the three flights of stairs we were all worn out. Moose, who was carrying both the footlocker and the largest suitcase, wasn't even winded.

If Moose was going to live with us, we were going to have to rearrange the furniture so we could get a third bed in what Miss Amanda Lewis would probably call "our darling little apartment." There was no way in the world we could have put two beds in one of the bedrooms, so we had to convert the study into a bedroom with two beds, and my bedroom into the study. If Number Three and I had had to do it ourselves, it would have taken us all night. But we had Moose now.

Number Three and I carried the frame of the extra bed up from the basement. Moose tagged along behind us. He carried the mattress under his right arm and the bedspring under the left. Then, while Number Three and I rested from our labor, Moose shifted the furniture around without so much as raising one drop of sweat.

And then two things happened almost at once. Moose sat down a little too heavily in our overstuffed chair, and the part that holds the cushion you sit on gave way. What I'm saying is that the bottom broke under the weight of Moose's bottom. He sank into the chair, in other words, and kept right on sinking. He opened his mouth and a roar that was part surprise and part displeasure came out.

At that exact moment The Thing came up the ladder, under what I thought of as the worst possible circumstances. That is, he had a bone the size of a two-by-four in his mouth. Now, there aren't very many bones that large around anywhere, and when The Thing got one, he quite naturally took pretty good care of it. What I mean to say is that when The Thing has got a bone like that, I never get near him unless I have my stuffed owl in my hand, and even then I'm a little uneasy.

So I would have been prepared to give pretty good odds that we were about to experience a major disaster. For one thing, as I've said, The Thing doesn't like to be surprised by finding strangers in what he thinks is his cell. For another, he had a really special bone in his jaws, and I knew that all he wanted to do was crawl into what he thinks of as his over-stuffed chair and eat it. It was what they call the worst possible combination of events. Not only was there a stranger in the cell when The Thing walked in with a special bone, but the stranger was in The Thing's overstuffed chair and making noises that practically any dog might mistake for a challenge to fight.

I jumped up from where I was sitting on the floor and ran to get my stuffed owl. By the time I got it, it was too late to do anything with it. The Thing had seen Moose in his overstuffed chair. He walked over to him, the bone still in his mouth. What I was think-ing was that I hoped The Thing would like living out in Colorado on the sheep ranch, and that it was go-ing to be pretty hard living in the cell with Moose after he came back from the hospital.

But it didn't happen that way at all. What hap-pened was that The Thing sat down on his haunches, dropped his bone in Moose's lap, and gave him his paw.

"Gee," Moose said, putting out his hand to The Thing before I could scream at him to stop. "A puppy!"

The Thing actually licked the hand Moose had stuck out. And then he got up on all fours again and leaned over and licked Moose on the forehead.

"Aww," Moose said, "what a sweet little puppy!"

Then he picked up The Thing's bone and threw it across the room and down the ladder. "Go get it, puppy dog." he ordered.

And so help me, The Thing went and got it for him. Up to then, I had felt pretty sure that whatever character traits Old English sheepdogs in general, and The Thing in particular, might have, retrieving wasn't one of them. Number Three and I had tried to teach him to fetch, of course. We would throw a stick or something and tell him to fetch, and all he would do was watch the stick go flying through the air and then look at us as if we were crazy. Number Three thought it was because of all the hair in his eyes, that he couldn't see the stick. But I knew that wasn't right. When he wanted to eat a football, he could see well enough to catch one in the air.

By the time The Thing chased the bone down the ladder and brought it back up, Moose had managed to unstick himself from the overstuffed chair he had sunk through. He was standing up when The Thing came back. The Thing dropped the bone at his feet and then stood up himself and put his paws on Moose's shoulders and licked his face.

"You guys have really got it made here," Moose said, "being allowed to keep a sweet little puppy like this right in your room."

The sweet little puppy then pushed on Moose a little harder than Moose expected, and Moose went over backward. The Thing stood over him and licked him some more. Getting licked by The Thing is like having a beach towel that somebody let go in the surf rubbed on you. It's that combination of wet and sand. Moose didn't seem to notice.

"You guys won't mind if I play with the puppy every once in a while, will you?" Moose asked.

"Our pleasure," Number Three and I said together.

"Great," Moose said. "Now can we go drive the go-cart?"

"Why don't we wait until tomorrow?" I replied.

"Because I want to go now," he said reasonably. He had just decided the desk would look better on the other side of the room and had picked it up to move it.

"Right," Number Three said.

"What if the track-and-field freaks are using the track?" I asked, not quite ready yet to give up.

"Why, I'm sure that if Moose asks them nicely," Number Three said, "they'll be willing to let him use the track."

"Yeah," Moose said.

"You have a point," I said, and pushed myself off the couch and followed Moose down the stairs. I thought that when I got to know Moose better, I would very politely suggest that he take the stairs one at a time. I didn't think the stairs were going to last long under the kind of pounding they were getting now, with his taking them three at a time.

Chapter 6

The go-carts were kept in a storage area under the concrete Elwood B. MacIntosh Memorial Grandstands. While Number Three and Moose were getting one of them out, I went over to where a couple of track-and-field freaks were standing on the cinder track. They had obviously been practicing jumping over those little fences, for the fences were in place on the track and they were in track uniform, but when I got there they were standing around in a circle talking excitedly.

"Here comes Pete," one of them said. "Hey, Pete,

did you hear what happened to Einstein Feinberg?"

Feinberg's real name is Stanley. They call him Einstein because he is a genius. He can stand up and argue calculus problems with the math instructor and win. He is also a champion chess player. The Catholic priest in town comes out to see Feinberg because Feinberg speaks better Latin than he does.

"No," I admitted. "I haven't heard what happened to him."

"He finally blew his cork," I was told. "Probably brain fever. That happens to people who spend all their time reading textbooks."

"What do you mean, he finally blew his cork?"

"He threw a football through Junior Ludwell's plate-glass window," the track-and-field freak said. "With Junior and his mate sitting right there on the porch."

"How do you know it was Einstein?" I asked.

"Because Junior ran off the porch and caught him, that's how," I was told.

"Caught him?"

"Yeah, he was the only guy on the street."

"Did he admit it?"

"That's what I mean when I said he finally blew his cork. Ludwell caught him, practically. There was nobody else in sight that could have thrown the ball. And Einstein looks him right in the eye and tells him he doesn't know anything about it."

Moose walked over. "Is it all right with you guys if I use the track to drive the go-cart?" he asked.

"We're practicing, fella!" one of the track-and-field freaks said, jerking his thumb toward the little fences on the cinder track.

"No, you're not," Moose said firmly. "You're standing around telling jokes to Pete."

"Look, fella," the freak said. "It took six of us a half an hour to put the jumps up. Now why should we take them down just because you want to play with a stupid go-cart?"

"I didn't ask you to help me," Moose said. "I'll get those little fences out of the way by myself."

Then he walked down the track, up to the two rows of little fences. He held his arms out by his sides, as if he were pretending to carry a tray or something. Then he started walking between the rows of jumps. He hooked each jump on his arm. When he had maybe four jumps on each arm, he went to the side of the track and set them down. Then he went and picked up another eight and put them on the side of the track. And then he did it a third time. It took him maybe ninety seconds, total.

The track-and-field freaks didn't like having their jumps taken off the track, but nobody said anything. They probably decided that since it was this six-foot-five-inch, two-hundred-and-sixty-pound boy's first day at school, they could afford to be nice to him.

I walked with Moose back to where Number Three was putting gasoline in the fuel tank of one of the go-carts.

"I think I'm going to like this," Moose said, wearing a smile from ear to ear. "How does it work?"

"It's very simple, actually," Number Three said. "That long pedal is the gas pedal. You step on that to make it go. The short, fat pedal is the brake pedal. You step on that to make it stop. You with me so far?"

"How come it's not making any noise?" Moose asked. *"Voom voom voom?"*

"That's because the engine's not running," Number Three explained.

"How do you turn the engine on?" Moose asked.

Number Three pointed out the starter, which is a length of rope with a little wooden handle on the end.

"You give that a quick, strong pull," Number Three explained. "And that starts the engine."

"Got you," Moose said. He bent over the engine, grabbed the starter rope, and gave it a quick, strong pull. There was a little popping noise. Moose looked at the short piece of rope in his hand. "It don't work," he said.

"The rope broke," I said. "Next time, don't pull it quite so hard."

"Does that mean I don't get to drive?" Moose asked.

"Not at all," Number Three said. "You can also start the engine by pushing the go-cart."

"Great," Moose said. He started to get in.

"I think it would probably be best if Number Three got in the cart and you pushed," I said.

"All right," Moose said reasonably. Number Three got behind the wheel. Moose put his hands on the back of the seat and started to push. For some reason the go-cart wouldn't start, although he pushed it maybe fifty feet. Then I realized what was wrong.

"Push it again, Moose," I said. "And this time don't lift the rear wheels off the ground."

"Got you," Moose said. This time he pushed downward. The engine popped, coughed, and finally caught. Number Three stopped the cart and got out, and Moose got behind the wheel.

"*Voom voom voom!*" he cried, and the go-cart started off, very slowly.

We stayed there, watching Moose drive around the cinder oval all by himself until it got too dark for him to see and he ran the go-cart into a water fountain. The Elwood B. MacIntosh Memorial Stadium is, like the catalogue advertises, lighted. There are big banks of electric lights mounted on the top of the grandstands and on a fence-type thing on the other side. But as our contribution to saving energy we don't turn them on anymore at night. Number Three says his father told him that in some ways the energy crisis might be a blessing in disguise, what with the cost of electricity these days.

When we got back to the cell, The Thing was lying on Moose's bed, working on the bone. When he saw Moose, he jumped off the bed and dropped the bone at his feet.

"Ain't that the sweetest thing you ever saw?" Moose asked, and picked The Thing up and cradled him in his arms like a baby. He even scratched The Thing's belly and went "itchy-kitchy-koo"! The Thing made noises of pleasure deep in his chest. If you didn't know The Thing, the noises of pleasure would have scared you out of two years' growth.

We stayed up pretty late that night, just talking. Moose confessed that he wasn't all that keen about coming to the Ludwell School but that his stepmother had insisted. She had been saying all along that the city was a jungle and no place to raise a child. Moose said that he had been able to talk his father out of sending him away to school until he got in trouble with the police in the park.

"What happened in the park, Moose?" Number Three asked.

"There were some guys teasing a little guy," Moose said. "A real little guy, no bigger than you, Runt. So I asked them to stop."

"And?" Number Three asked.

"The one I threw in the model-sailboat pond made so much noise the cops came," Moose said. "He didn't have to make all that noise, screaming for help the way he did. You'd have to work at it to drown in that model-sailboat pond, it's only a couple of feet deep."

"You got arrested?" I asked, fascinated.

"Detained," he explained.

"I don't understand," I said. "What's the difference?"

"You have to be sixteen to be arrested. Same cell, but there's some kind of a difference."

"You got detained for throwing the guy in the lake?" Number Three asked.

"No, I was detained for throwing the cop in the sailboat pond."

"Why did you throw the cop in the pond?"

"He wanted to take me down to the station house to call my parents. I told him he didn't have to do that, I was on my way home for supper anyway, and I'd tell them what happened myself. But he insisted, and started to push me toward the police car, and the first thing I think I knew, there he was in the sailboat pond, with some kid screaming because he'd landed on his boat."

"If he was in the pond," I asked, "how did he detain you?"

"He went and got four more cops. I still don't know how they knew where I lived. But anyway, they came by the apartment while we were having supper. The one I threw in the pond didn't believe my father when my father said I was only thirteen. That made my father mad, of course, not being believed, so he said something to the cops that really made *them* mad, and they arrested him. By the time my father's lawyer got us out of the police station, my stepmother was hysterical, and here I am."

"That's a sad story, Moose," Number Three said.

"Ah, maybe it won't be so bad. What with the sweet little puppy to play with and the go-carts to practice on, it may not be as bad as it looks around here."

"Pete's got stepmother problems, too," Number Three said.

"No fooling?" Moose said. "Sorry about that, Runt. I know how it is."

"Pete's father is going to marry a stewardess," Number Three said. "And then Pete's going to go live with them in Florida. In an old funeral home."

"Well, isn't that a coincidence?" Moose said. "You're going to have a stewardess for a stepmother, and your father's in the same profession as mine."

"Mine's an engineer," I said. "A construction engineer. Is that what yours is?"

"No. When Number Three said that about the

79

funeral home, I thought you meant your father was in the funeral-home profession, like mine."

"Your father's an undertaker?"

"Yeah," Moose said, blushing modestly. "My father is J. Monroe Hanrahan, Sr., of Hanrahan's Memorial Mansions. We have six memorial mansions offering complete memorial services to fit any pocketbook."

"I seem to remember seeing the billboards," I said.

"But your stepmother is a stewardess?" Number Three asked. Since he has only the original set of parents, he is naturally curious about those of us who have picked up others along the way.

"Not this one," Moose said. "The one before the last one. She was a stewardess. The last one was a lady who sold casket mattresses. My father met her at a funeral directors' convention. The one he's got now he met professionally."

"You mean she's also an undertaker?" Number Three asked.

"No, I mean he met her when he buried her husband. I think he gave her a professional discount on the casket to get to know her better. It doesn't really matter, though, stepmothers are pretty much all alike. You know that, Runt."

"No, I don't, either," I said. "This will be my first one."

"No fooling? And you're starting off with a stewardess? Boy, that's bad news!" Moose really felt sorry for me, and on that cheerful note we finally went to sleep.

The sacred motto of the Ludwell dining hall, "Take All You Want, But Eat All You Take," had been written with economy, and not Moose Hanrahan, in mind. For breakfast he had six eggs, a half-dozen pancakes, a dozen link sausages, and about a pound of bacon, and he washed it all down with four glasses of orange juice and five half-pint containers of milk.

I was so fascinated watching him eat that I didn't see Junior Ludwell leave the faculty dining table and walk over to where we sat until he laid a friendly hand on my shoulder.

I had expected to see Junior today. But I hadn't expected the smile and the friendly hand on my shoulder. If I was a betting man, which I am, I would have given odds of three to one that by noon today Junior would have figured out that Einstein Feinberg hadn't tossed the football through his plate-glass window, and that I would get blamed for it.

"Good morning, Rutherford, James, and Monroe," Junior said. "And how are you all today?" Probably because he didn't really care how we all were today, he went on without waiting for our answer. "Rutherford, on your way to class, would you please stop by the field house and see Coach Ramsey? He sent word he wants to see you."

"Yes, sir," I said.

"We have a little rule here, Monroe," Junior said. He had seen Moose take another table-sized stack of pancakes from a passing student waiter. "Take all you want, but eat all you take."

"It don't work," Moose said.

"What do you mean, it don't . . ." He corrected himself, "*doesn't* work?"

"They ran out of bacon," Moose said, holding up the empty bacon tray as proof.

"Well, yes," Junior said. "Indeed. Well, I expect you'd better be finishing up and getting ready for class." He patted me on the shoulder and walked away.

On my way to the field house, which from the dining hall is in the opposite direction from Prouter Hall, where my math class was scheduled, I saw that we had something new on the campus. Mr. Davis was riding it. For a minute I couldn't figure out what it was. It looked like a little tractor, except that the wheels were all of the same size, and I couldn't see anything on it that looked like it would cut grass. It had a huge plastic bag on the back. I caught up with Mr. Davis and his machine when he stopped by a wagon.

"Good morning, Mr. Davis," I said. "Exactly what is that thing you're riding?"

"You know exactly what it is, Runt Peters," Mr. Davis said. "And if you think you're going to get anywhere near it, you've got another think coming."

He got off the machine, went to the back of it, and unhooked the plastic bag. He dumped the bag on the wagon. The bag was full of grass clippings and twigs.

"What is that, some sort of vacuum cleaner?" I asked.

"It's a professional-model grounds sweeper, is what it is," Mr. Davis said proudly. "And you and Junior Ludwell's kid aren't going to get anywhere near it."

Mr. Davis had been at the Ludwell School, in charge of grounds maintenance, since the school was founded. He had known our beloved headmaster, in other words, since Mr. Ludwell had been in short pants and was called Junior by our beloved founder. Mr. Davis was getting on in years, as they say, and he generally wiped out at least one major piece of grounds-keeping machinery a year. Last spring, before he ran it into a tree, he drove one side of a brand-new commercial lawn mower over Mrs. Ludwell's tulip beds. Number Three said that was the first time he had ever heard his mother say a naughty word.

I was surprised, after that and several other incidents, that they had bought him a new machine. With Number Three and me and the other unpatriotic, non-football-playing criminals pushing lawn mowers, there was no need to replace the commercial lawn mower. Then I got a good look at his new machine. It wasn't as powerful as it seemed. There was a metal tag bolted to the engine which proudly announced it was a full 7.5 horsepower. That was only about twice as powerful as the engines on the go-carts. Even Mr. Davis couldn't get in much trouble with a 7.5-horsepower machine.

I waved good-bye to him, he told me to get lost, and I walked on to the field house for my meeting with Coach Ramsey.

Coach Ramsey, who has long, silver, curly hair, goes around dressed in a sweatshirt, a baseball cap, and a whistle on a cord around his neck. I like him all right, but he is not what you could call one of my admirers. So far as he is concerned, anybody who doesn't go out for football with a big smile is probably in the employ of a foreign power, like Russia. I had no idea what he wanted with me.

"I heard about the football and the plate-glass window," he said, without any greeting first, when I walked into his office.

"It's hard to believe Einstein Feinberg would do something like that, isn't it?" I said. "It goes to show you can never tell about people, doesn't it?"

"I said I heard about it," Coach Ramsey said. "By that, I mean how it *really* happened."

"Oh," I said.

"I'll put it to you straight, Peters," Coach Ramsey said. "The Lions really need him on the team."

"Einstein Feinberg?"

"Einstein Feinberg is as useless as you are," Coach Ramsey said. "I'm talking about Moose Hanrahan, and you know it."

"Yes, sir. But Moose doesn't want to play football, Coach."

"I don't care if he wants to play football or not," Coach Ramsey said. "I'm sick and tired of our unbroken record of lost football games. As far as I'm concerned, Moose Hanrahan is a gift from heaven, and I'm not going to see a future All-American tackle wasting his time cutting grass with you and Junior Ludwell's kid."

"I don't see how you're going to talk him into playing, Coach," I said. "Once Moose makes up his mind . . ."

"I'm not going to talk him into playing," Coach Ramsey said. "*You* are."

"How am I going to do that?"

"You'll think of something," Coach Ramsey said. "Talk it over with Ludwell the Third. Considering the alternative, I think you'll be able to talk Moose into playing."

"What alternative?"

"What kind of cheerleaders do you think the two of you would make?" Coach Ramsey said.

"But the Ludwell School has never had cheerleaders," I said.

"Not so far, we haven't," Coach Ramsey said. "The way I see it, Peters, is that we dress you and Ludwell the Third up in lion suits. How does that sound?"

"Coach Ramsey, you wouldn't!"

"With sort of a shaggy yellow beard around the face," Coach Ramsey said. "And a long, long tail, with a little ball of yellow fur at the end."

"I'll see what I can do," I said.

"Have him here for practice at half-past three," Coach Ramsey said.

Chapter 7

The next thing I had to do, of course, was lie. It was a desperate situation. I had wide-awake nightmares in which Number Three and I were out in front of the grandstands dressed up in lion suits, complete with a yellow beard around the face and a long tail.

What I did was go to Einstein Feinberg and tell him that Coach Ramsey had said that unless Moose played football there would be *three* cheerleaders, the third one named Stanley Feinberg.

"I don't trust you, Peters," Einstein Feinberg said.

"Why not, Stanley?"

"You want something from me. Otherwise you'd

be calling me Einstein like the rest of the mental midgets around here do."

"All right, Einstein," I said. "Have it your way. Maybe I'm wrong. Now that I think of it, you're probably the kind of guy who'll be perfectly happy dressed up in a lion suit, jumping up and down in front of a stadium full of people."

Einstein Feinberg stared at me for a full thirty seconds from behind his glasses. Then he said, "On the other hand, we do seem to be in this difficult situation together, don't we?"

"You bet we do," I said. "What are we going to do about it?"

Einstein looked thoughtful. His eyes sort of glassed over for a moment. The computer between his ears was obviously at work. "It's a simple question of supply and demand," he said finally.

"Huh?"

"We have to offer this muscle-bound pal of yours something in exchange for his services on the football team," Einstein said.

"Like what?"

"What, for example, does he like to do?" he asked.

"He likes to drive go-carts," I said.

"You're kidding."

"I wouldn't kid at a time like this," I said.

"Okay, then," Einstein said. "We tell him that

unless he plays football and gets us off the hook, he can't drive a go-cart anymore."

"Who's going to tell Moose Hanrahan he can't drive a go-cart?" I asked. "Not me, Einstein."

"You probably have a point," Einstein said. His eyes glassed over again for a moment. He had turned his computer on again. "Okay," he said. "So what's better than go-cart driving?"

"I can think of a lot of things," I said, "none of which are going to appeal to Moose. So far as Moose is concerned, happiness is going *voom voom voom* around the track."

"Go-cart *racing* is better than go-cart *driving*," Einstein Feinberg explained patiently.

"Who's he going to race?" I asked.

"You, me, and Number Three," Einstein said. "And guess who's going to win?"

I read somewhere that the test of genius is to find a simple solution to a complex problem. I was proud of myself for coming to Einstein for the solution to my problem.

"You really think he'd go for it, Einstein?"

"There's only one way to find out," Einstein said. "Let's ask him."

When the last class of the day was over, Einstein, Number Three, and I found Moose Hanrahan where we knew he would be. He was going *voom voom*

voom around the cinder track while the track-and-field freaks stood watching him. They had talked about complaining to Junior Ludwell about not being able to use the track to jump over their little fences, but they couldn't get a volunteer to do the actual complaining. Moose was liable to find out who had complained.

He finally ran out of gas, and Einstein, Number Three, and I went over to where the go-cart had stopped.

"It don't work," Moose said glumly. He nudged the go-cart with his toe and sent it sliding six feet.

"Out of gas," Number Three said. "I'll get some for you in a minute, Moose. But first we have an idea for you."

Moose didn't respond to that. Instead he looked at Einstein. "You must be Feinberg," he said.

"That's right," Einstein said, surprised. "How did you know?"

"When I asked if there was anybody around here who could play a good game of chess, they told me there was only one guy, name of Feinberg."

"But how did you know I was Feinberg?" Einstein asked.

"They said you looked like an underfed crow with glasses," Moose said.

"You play chess, Moose?" Number Three asked. If he was looking around for somebody who could play a good game of chess, it would seem likely that he played the game himself, as out of character as that seemed for Moose. Number Three sounded as surprised as I was.

"My father got one of the embalmers to teach me how," Moose said.

"One of the embalmers?" I asked.

"You know what an embalmer is?" Moose asked. "He's the guy who . . ."

"I know, I know," I said quickly.

"Then why do you sound so surprised?" Moose said.

"I just never put embalming and chess together before, I suppose," I said.

"The thing is," Moose explained, seeing that I was a little confused, "the funeral business is a little different from most other businesses. I mean, you can't build up an inventory. Embalmers have to wait until the business comes their way, you see what I mean?"

"Yeah," I said. "I see your point."

"So while they're hanging around the preparation room, waiting for business, they have to have something to pass the time. Their union won't let them wash the hearses or cut the grass. All they can do is embalm. And there's not enough of them — just one, ordinarily, unless there's a lot of business — to get up a card game. So the way they usually pass the time is playing chess with the casket salesmen.

They have the same kind of problem, I mean about waiting for business to come their way. They can hardly go around drumming up business by knocking on doors and asking people if they want to buy a casket. You know what I mean?"

"I got it," I said.

"I've been playing chess since I was six," Moose went on. "Ever since my father decided that my riding my tricycle around the viewing rooms was bad for business and he turned me over to the embalmers," Moose said. "What happened was that I went riding into the George Washington Room just as they were rolling somebody out to the hearse. I didn't run into the casket or anything, but I did sort of roll into the monsignor who was leading the way, and he got pretty mad at my father. Anyway, after that I got turned over to the embalmer, and he taught me how to play chess." Moose looked at me. I could tell he had just thought of something. "You're not hinting there's anything sissy about playing chess, are you, Runt?"

"Of course not," I said immediately.

"Sometimes people figure that if you spend a lot of time around a funeral home and get in the habit of not talking loud and spend a lot of time playing chess, you must be a sissy," Moose went on. I had the feeling that he didn't like people who came to that conclusion.

"It was the furthest thing from Runt's mind, Moose," Number Three said, coming to my aid. "Some of our best friends, like Feinberg here, play chess."

"About this idea of ours, Moose," I said.

"What idea?"

"How does go-cart racing strike you?" I asked.

"I was thinking about that myself," Moose said. "It's already getting a little dull, going *voom voom voom* in circles all by myself. When do we start?"

I was suddenly struck with an inspiration.

"There's one small problem," I said.

"Like what?" Moose asked, suspiciously.

"We need a racecourse," I said.

"What's wrong with this place?"

"Well, there's two things wrong with it," I said. "First, the track-and-field freaks want to use it."

"So what?" Moose replied. "They can jump over their little fences when we're finished."

"And second, what we need is a real racecourse."

"Where are you going to get a real racecourse?" he asked.

"We'll mark one out on the grounds," I said. "Say from here around the lake, and then over to the library and past the residence hall, and finally back here."

"What makes you think they'd let us do that?" Moose asked.

"Well, I'm sure they'd be willing to do us a favor if we did them a favor," I said.

"I smell a rat, Runt," Moose said. "You're talking about my going out for football, aren't you?"

"To be perfectly honest with you, Moose, yes, I am," I said, and held my breath.

Moose's eyes glassed over, just like Einstein's eyes glassed over when he was thinking. I finally realized that Moose was thinking, too.

"Okay," he said. "I'll tell you what I'm going to do. You get your racecourse set up, and I'll play football."

"Great!" I said. "I was sure you could see the logic of my proposal. Coach Ramsey is waiting for you at the field house to give you your uniform."

"I won't need the uniform until the game," Moose said. "The game isn't till Saturday. I'll pick it up sometime between now and then."

"But what about practice?" I said.

"What about it?" Moose replied. "I said I'd play football, provided you set up a racecourse. I didn't say anything about practice."

"You might as well," I said, trying to sound reasonable. "There won't be anything else for you to do anyway, while Number Three, Einstein, and I are setting up the racecourse."

"Yeah, there will," Moose said. "Stanley and I

can play chess." He looked at Einstein. "They were wrong about you," he said.

"They were?" Einstein asked.

"Yeah, you look more like an owl than a crow."

"I was really hoping to see Moose Hanrahan walk through that door," Coach Ramsey said when I walked into his office. "What size lion suit did you say you wear?"

"I don't really think we're going to need the lion suits, Coach," I said.

"I told you, Peters," he said. "It's either Moose Hanrahan or the lion suits, and you don't look anything like Moose Hanrahan. Where is he?"

"As a matter of fact, Coach," I said, "he's playing chess with Einstein Feinberg."

"Well, I'll say this for you, Peters. You really have a good imagination when it comes to excuses. Did you really expect me to believe that?"

"It's the absolute, unvarnished truth," I said. "Haven't you ever heard that truth is stranger than fiction?"

"What is it, another one of Feinberg's psychological experiments?" Coach Ramsey asked.

"Oh, I don't think so," I said, trying to sound confident and reassuring. It had occurred to me that

Coach Ramsey might be on to something.

"I remember the time he tried to talk me into letting him hypnotize the basketball team," Coach Ramsey went on. "I don't like to talk about the boys, but have you ever thought, Runt, that Einstein Feinberg is a little weird?"

"I hadn't heard about Einstein hypnotizing the basketball team," I said.

"Oh, yeah," Coach Ramsey said. "I knew all along, of course, that it wouldn't work, and I should have known better than to let him try. All it did was make them run funny. They didn't play one little bit better hypnotized than they did wide awake. But we're not talking about the basketball team, Runt, we're talking about the football team. And we're specifically talking about my expecting to see Moose Hanrahan, not you, walk in my door."

"I told you, Coach, he's playing chess with Einstein Feinberg."

"That's going to do us a lot of good when we play Barton Academy," Coach Ramsey said. "They're coming over here to play football, not chess. They're coming over here to give us another shameful beating at football, to put a point on it. The only way we can keep them from doing that, again, is if we get Moose Hanrahan out there on the field."

"Moose Hanrahan will be in uniform for the Barton game, Coach," I said. "Ready, and I might even say eager, to play."

He looked at me a little suspiciously. "Say that again?" he asked.

"Provided, of course, that we can do him a little favor."

"What kind of a little favor?" Coach Ramsey asked, very suspiciously.

I told him about Moose wanting to race go-carts. I must say he took it very well.

"I'll put my cards on the table, Peters," he said. "After I heard what Moose did with the football, I took the whole team over to the residence hall to see how many of them could throw the ball over the roof. You know what happened?"

"No, sir."

"Don't ask," he said, shaking his head as if to clear it of a painful memory. "I'm desperate. If setting up a go-cart racecourse is what it's going to take to get Moose Hanrahan in uniform for the game against Barton, he gets a go-cart racecourse."

"That's very generous of you, Coach Ramsey."

"No, it's not. It's just that I don't have the courage to face Coach Stevens again. If there's one thing I can't stand, it is to have someone pity me."

There were a few little problems that remained to be ironed out. For one thing, Coach Ramsey insisted that Moose practice with the Ludwell Lions before the Barton game.

"Look at it this way, Peters," he said. "I know that Moose Hanrahan is the best thing that's happened to the Ludwell Lions since I came here to coach. But just as you and Ludwell the Third couldn't go out there in your lion suits to lead the cheering without practice, neither can good old Moose go out there and win one for us without, say, four days' practice."

"Maybe I could talk him into practicing on Thursday afternoon," I said.

"Three days' practice, as an absolute minimum," Coach Ramsey replied.

"I'm not even sure I can get him to practice on Thursday," I said.

"Thursday and Friday," Coach Ramsey said. "That's my final offer. It's either Thursday and Friday, or you and Ludwell the Third can start practicing right now how not to step on your lion-suit tails."

"It'll have to be Wednesday and Thursday," I said.

"Why not Friday?"

"Friday is when we told him we would hold the go-cart races," I said.

"Who's he going to race?" Coach Ramsey asked.

"Number Three, Einstein Feinberg, and me," I said. "Who else?"

"What kind of competition is that?" Coach Ramsey asked, horrified. "What kind of a taste of victory is good old Moose going to get from beating the three of you?"

"I don't quite know what you mean, Coach," I said.

"I'll tell you what I'm going to do," Coach Ramsey said, "just to show you that my heart's in the right place. He can race against the guys on the team. They won't like having to get in those fool cars, but they're prepared to make whatever sacrifices are necessary for the good of the team. Which is more than I can say for some people, like you."

"I'm not so sure that's a good idea," I said.

"Why not?"

"What if they beat him?" I asked.

"What if they do?" he replied. "There always has to be a winner and a loser, Peters. That's what sports is all about."

"If Moose loses, he may not be in a very good mood to play football against Barton," I said. "He takes go-carts very seriously."

"You should have thought of that before," Coach Ramsey said.

"Oh, we did. We had that all figured out," I said.

"What were you going to do?"

"Let me put it this way, Coach," I said. "Moose wasn't going to lose."

"You mean you were going to throw the race? Cheat to let him win?" There was a tone of absolute horror in his voice.

"Not *cheat*, exactly," I said. "We thought of it as driving very discreetly."

"I see," he said coldly. "Well, let *me* put it to *you* this way, Peters. The guys on my team don't play the game that way. No matter what the name of the game is, football or go-cart racing, my guys go in there to win!"

"You mean you won't even suggest to them that the way to make Moose a happy football player is to let him win at driving go-carts?"

"Absolutely not!" he said. "Look at it like this. Anybody who can throw a football over a three-story building and through a plate-glass window on the next block has to be a first-class athlete, right?"

"Right."

"And go-cart racing is just another form of athletics, right?"

I didn't quite agree with that, but I had learned a long time ago never to argue with Coach Ramsey when he was giving a pep talk.

"Right," I said.

"So it just stands to reason that good old Moose will win anyway," he said.

"If you say so," I said.

"So there will be no more talk about cheating,"

Coach Ramsey said. "You and Ludwell the Third just make sure that good old Moose is happy after the go-cart race. You understand me?"

"To do that, we're probably going to have to cheat," I said.

"I don't ever want to hear you use that word again!" Coach Ramsey said. "Now get out of here!"

Chapter 8

When I left Coach Ramsey's office I went to see Mr. Davis. Mr. Davis has an apartment over the garage in what Junior Ludwell calls the Grounds Maintenance Building. The building isn't as large as the garage behind the house in Florida that Miss Amanda Lewis wanted my father to buy so we could live in it after they got married, but it is big enough for the Ludwell School pickup truck, the professional-model grounds sweeper, our lawn mowers, and things like that. Out in back is the greenhouse, which is nothing more than the frame of a building with plastic sheeting draped over it. I was here two years before I realized that Mr. Davis's greenhouse is the Ludwell School Botanical Garden & Laboratory mentioned in the catalogue.

Mr. Davis was an important, if unwitting, part of the equation that was going to keep Coach Ramsey from dressing Number Three and me up in cheerleaders' lion suits by getting Moose Hanrahan to play football by giving him a chance to race go-carts.

The nearer I got to the Grounds Maintenance Building, the less likely it seemed to me that Mr. Davis was going to go along with our setting up a racecourse on the campus. He gets pretty excited sometimes when people just walk on his grass. "Walkways are for walking" is his motto; "grass is for looking." After all the years Mr. Davis had spent growing grass, fertilizing it, mowing it, and sweeping up the crop, it seemed very unlikely that he was going to stand still as we turned part of it into a go-cart racecourse, even for a very good cause.

Mr. Davis wasn't at the Grounds Maintenance Building when I got there. It was a good thing he wasn't, for although I am usually able to argue one side of a question as well as the other, I really couldn't think of an opening argument, much less a closing one, to use on him.

I could faintly hear the sound of his professional-model grounds sweeper coming from somewhere down by the lake, which meant that he was out giving his grass his usual tender loving care. There was nothing to do but wait for him. Even though the situation looked pretty hopeless, the only choice I had was between asking him and *probably* getting laughed at, and not asking him, which meant the cheerleaders' lion suits and *certainly* getting laughed at.

But then, just like Junior Ludwell is always saying, perseverance in the face of overwhelming adversity pays off. I saw what just could be a solution to the problem. What I saw were Mrs. Ludwell's tulip-bed warning flags. There were about two hundred of them, wrapped up in bundles of maybe ten each, stacked against the wall beside some bags of fertilizer.

The year before a salesman had left Mr. Davis a new kind of lawn mower to try out. It had been designed for use in modern cemeteries, the kind where the tombstones are made of metal and laid flat on the ground instead of out of marble and standing up. The salesman told Mr. Davis it was a revolutionary breakthrough in grounds-keeping technology and he felt sure that it would work at least as well on the Ludwell campus as it would in a modern cemetery. He pointed out that we didn't even have laid-flat tombstones.

What it was was a little tractor that pulled what looked like eight push-type lawn mowers hooked up side by side. You know the kind I mean, the ones with curving blades instead of one blade that goes around in a circle lopping off the grass. The ones on the machine didn't have handles, of course, since the tractor was going to drag them around instead of somebody pushing on them.

Well, Mr. Davis was pretty excited about a lawn mower that could cut a twenty-foot-wide piece of grass all at once, and cut it just as close and evenly as if each of those eight spin-around lawn mowers had been pushed by somebody. Mr. Davis was a firm believer in the spin-around type of lawn mower as opposed to the one-big-blade-turning-around type. For one thing, the turn-around types have a habit of throwing all the grass they cut in little piles out on one side, while the spin-around types just chop it up in little pieces and sort of spread the cut-off grass around evenly.

Well, the new lawn mower worked all right at first — just perfectly, as a matter of fact. We all went out to watch this revolutionary breakthrough in grounds-keeping technology. The tractor had a self-starter, which was an obvious technological advantage over those little ropes with a handle that you had to pull on to get the engine going. Mr. Davis got it going. He drove it over to where the grass starts next to the parking lot by the Grounds Maintenance Building. So far, the eight lawn mowers hitched up behind it were up in the air. Then Mr. Davis moved a lever and they went down on the grass. And the minute he got the whole thing going forward, the lawn mowers started to spin around and cut grass.

Mr. Davis drove it maybe twenty feet and then stopped. He got off the tractor and went and looked at the grass it had cut. It had done everything that the salesman had said it would, and, as anybody who has ever dealt with a salesman knows, that doesn't always happen. Not only was the grass cut as short and evenly as it is when you use a spin-around, push-type lawn mower, but the cut-off grass had been chopped up in little tiny pieces and spread neatly, not thrown off to one side in an unsightly pile that would turn brown and have to be picked up.

Mr. Davis, who had been examining the cut grass very closely, got up, brushed the grass off his knees, and got back on the tractor. Everybody applauded, which Mr. Davis was not used to, and which might well explain what happened next. He drove from the Grounds Maintenance Building parking lot up toward the stadium, looking behind him every once in a while to make sure that everything was working the way it should. Then he came to a tree, one of those trees the catalogue calls "our stately oaks." Well, he just drove around the tree the way he always drove around trees on his old riding lawn mower, this time carefully making allowance for the ten feet of lawn mowers sticking out on the left-hand side. But in the excitement of the moment he forgot that he was also dragging ten feet of lawn mowers on the right side. That put him twenty feet to the right of the tree, and the right-hand ten feet of spin-around lawn mowers rolled right through one of Mrs. Ludwell's tulip beds and wiped it out.

Mrs. Ludwell saw what was happening, of course, and she yelled at him, and Mr. Davis heard her, but I guess he was still pretty confused about having been applauded before and thought that she was just encouraging him some more. So he just waved at her, and instead of making a U-turn around the oak tree he decided to cut the grass along the road that leads from Headmaster's House to the lake. That road, which was lined on both sides by Mrs. Ludwell's tulip beds, is sort of our *piece de resistance* so far as campus roads go, and he was probably thinking he was doing her a favor.

He steered carefully right alongside the tulip bed, the way he always did on his riding lawn mower, and kept looking over his left shoulder to make sure the lawn mowers were still working the way they were supposed to. If he had looked over his right shoulder, he would have seen that the right-hand mowers were rolling over Mrs. Ludwell's tulips.

As a matter of fact, Mr. Davis didn't realize what had been happening until he got to where the road curves away from the lake. He tried to make a U-turn and the right-hand half of the lawn mowers ran into another tree. That made enough noise to make him look over his right shoulder for the first time to see what had happened.

Even then he didn't understand what he had done to Mrs. Ludwell's tulip beds. She had caught up to him by then, but she was sort of out of breath and excited, and what he thought she was so mad about was his breaking the right-hand lawn mowers up against the stately oak.

Right after that, when it looked as if the school were going to have to buy the lawn mower because the salesman could hardly sell it to someone else with the three right-hand mowers all bent out of shape, Junior Ludwell ordered the tulip-bed warning flags. What they are are four-foot-tall iron stakes. On the top of each stake is a little flag, shaped like a triangle and made of nylon. They are what they call international distress orange in color. That's an orange so bright it hurts your eyes when you look at it too long.

The idea was that if the school had to buy the twenty-foot-wide cemetery-type lawn mower, Mrs. Ludwell would put the flags out around her tulip beds so that Mr. Davis would remember how wide the lawn mower is. As it happened, the school didn't have to buy the cemetery-model lawn mower. All we had to do was pay for the damage.

At about that time, probably because what happened made him think about having the grass cut, Junior Ludwell got the bright idea that putting the hardened criminals to work cutting the grass with push-type lawn mowers would not only keep us occupied but save gas and flowerbeds and bushes as well. So the flags were never used.

When I saw them, I was struck with another one of my inspirations. I was a little embarrassed about not having thought of it before, for there was the solution to my problem, as plain as the nose on my face.

I had been thinking about a *permanent* racecourse. There was no way Mr. Davis was going to let me build a permanent racecourse on his grass. But a *temporary* racecourse was something else. All we had to do was mark out a course with the tulip-bed warning flags by sticking them in the grass just before the race. As soon as the race was over we could pull them out. Unless you looked closely, there would be no way to tell that there ever had been a racecourse.

What would happen if Mr. Davis came along during the race was something I didn't want to think about right then. So that I could show Number Three and Einstein Feinberg what I was talking about, I grabbed one bundle of tulip-bed warning flags and started to leave the Grounds Maintenance Building. At that moment Mr. Davis rolled up on his professional-model grounds sweeper.

"Where do you think you're going with Mrs. Ludwell's tulip flags?" he asked, jumping off the grounds sweeper. After the fuss Mrs. Ludwell had caused after he had wiped out her tulips, it was understandable that Mr. Davis thought of the flags as "Mrs. Ludwell's tulip flags," even though they weren't really hers. But what he called them gave me another idea. Sometimes the way my imagination comes to help me when I'm in trouble is really amazing.

"Marking out possible tulip beds," I said.

"What's that supposed to mean?" he asked.

"Well, you know how badly Mrs. Ludwell felt after the tulip accident," I said.

"Those things happen," Mr. Davis said. "I never said I never make a mistake."

"Well," I said, "she's thinking of putting in replacement tulip beds."

"Where?"

"We don't know yet," I said. "We're going to mark off possible places to put tulip beds, with the flags. She can make up her mind where she actually wants to put them after she sees all the possible places."

"Sounds nutty to me," Mr. Davis said. "Why doesn't she put them back where she had them?"

"You know what happened there," I said.

110

He thought that over for a minute. "Just make sure you put them flags back when she's finished," Mr. Davis said. Then he got back on his professional-model grounds sweeper and drove it into the garage.

I went back to the residence hall, and as I started up the ladder to the cell I heard Moose Hanrahan's happy voice.

"Checkmate, Four-Eyes!" he boomed cheerfully.

When I actually got to the cell, I found Moose and Einstein Feinberg sitting on the floor with a chess-board between them. The Thing was lying next to Moose, contentedly gnawing on a football he had caught somewhere.

"You want another game?" Moose asked.

"Not today," Einstein said. "Suffering four such humiliating defeats sequentially is quite sufficient for one day."

I told myself there was no reason I should be surprised that Einstein Feinberg had figured out himself that the way to keep Moose happy was to let him win at chess. I winked at him.

"I know what your devious mind presumes the case to be, Peters," Einstein said. "And you're wrong."

"What's he thinking?" Moose asked. "And what are those flags for?"

"They're to mark off the racecourse," I replied. I was hoping desperately that Einstein, who has an

111

awful habit of always telling the truth, would not tell Moose what he knew I had been thinking.

"No fooling?" Moose said, jumping to his feet. "Let me see one."

"Moose," Einstein Feinberg said, putting out his hand, "you're the best chess player I've ever had the privilege of playing against. It is a pleasure to lose to someone like you."

"Ah, you ain't so bad yourself, Four-Eyes," Moose said graciously. "You keep at it, and you'll get better." He actually blushed. I wondered how much blood it took to turn a head that large bright red.

"I'd like to talk to you a moment, Peters," Einstein said. "Walk me back to my cell."

"Okay," I said. I had no idea what he would want to talk to me about, especially in private. Einstein normally stuck to himself. It wasn't that he didn't like people, or that people didn't like him. It was just that he was so smart that the rest of us bored him. His idea of a great time was to read a book about a Greek philosopher in Latin. The only reason we were friends at all is that, for different reasons, of course, neither one of us was in what Junior Ludwell called the Ludwell Mainstream. That, and the fact that Einstein and The Thing liked each other. I don't know how that started, either, but that's the way it was. If The Thing wasn't in our cell or with his private garbage can behind the dining hall, you could count on finding him in Feinberg's cell. Feinberg couldn't play his violin concertos on his stereo when The Thing was there, because The Thing thought he was supposed to sing along with the violin, but even that didn't seem to bother Einstein much. When The Thing was visiting, Einstein just read a book or something and let The Thing eat stuff from his regular, once-a-week food package from his stepmother.

When we got to Einstein's cell, he closed the door behind us and offered me a chair.

"I've been having second thoughts about what we're doing," Feinberg said.

"What are we doing?" I asked.

"Taking advantage of Moose Hanrahan's good nature for our personal advantage," Einstein said. "It's not right."

"I don't think many people take advantage of Moose Hanrahan," I said. "Particularly people who don't weigh a hundred pounds soaking wet. No offense, Einstein."

"Perhaps you will feel differently if I tell you what we talked about when you were over stealing the tulip-bed warning flags," Einstein said.

"So tell me, and I'll decide," I said.

"We were talking about you. What I mean to say is that Moose brought the subject of you and your stewardess up. Moose is very concerned about that."

"It's not my stewardess, it's my father's stewardess, and it's none of your business, or Moose's either."

"Moose is very grateful to you for the way you and Number Three have treated him," Einstein said. "He thinks of himself as your friend, and that gives him the right to worry about your stewardess. And me, too, Rutherford."

"I keep telling you, it's my father's stewardess, and there's not a thing to worry about."

"Your argument, Peters, like most of your arguments, is based on a position that I will charitably call innocence. Some people would call it ignorance. You quite obviously don't know a thing about stewardii."

"And I suppose you do?"

"Moose and I both know a great deal more about stewardii than you do."

"Moose maybe does," I said. "Moose once had one for a stepmother. But what experience, except for having one dump a bowl of soup in your lap on an airplane, do you have? I know for a fact that after your mother died, your father married her sister. You're not going to try to tell me that your aunt and/or stepmother was a stewardess, are you?"

Mrs. Feinberg, like most splendid cooks I have met, was a shade on the far side of what you could call pleasingly plump. While I liked her very much, the cold fact was that she wasn't the sort of lady whose picture the airline would put on a billboard to encourage people to fly. To come to supper, maybe, but not to fly.

"Do you ever wonder about my father, Peters?" Einstein asked.

"Wonder what about your father?"

"I suppose you've been able to guess he has a very successful and lucrative practice of law?"

"I sort of figured that out when I saw him driving that Rolls-Royce convertible," I said.

"Do you know what kind of a law practice he has?" Einstein asked, and then went on without waiting for me to reply. "A *stewardii* practice, that's what kind."

"I don't know what you're talking about," I said.

"That's what I mean about your innocence," Einstein said. "Let me enlighten you. Your stewardess is not the first one who has become infatuated with an older man with graying temples, a certain world-traveler's *savoir-faire*, and a lot of money. And vice versa."

"What are you leading up to, Einstein?" I asked.

"It happens all the time," Einstein went on. "If you'd ever read anything but the funny papers, you would know that every young girl dreams of meeting a handsome, successful man with a lot of money. By the time they become stewardii and have been carrying trays for a couple of months, they're willing to forget the handsome part. And you know what every man dreams about: having some nice-looking girl fuss over him. Bring him a cup of coffee, put a pillow behind his head, bring him a magazine, that sort of thing."

"I'm not sure I like what you're saying, Stanley," I said.

"So you put the two together on an airplane, and what do you have? Instant infatuation. She looks at him and decides that not only here is the man she's been waiting for all her life, but once she gets to marry him, she can stop being an airborne waitress. For the man it's much the same thing. Even though, having been married, he should know better, what he sees in the stewardess is still something he's been waiting for all his life. A good-looking woman to bring him his coffee and his newspapers and to smile at him a lot. That's where my father comes in."

"What do you mean by that?"

"Sometimes he gets called in early, which means breach of promise. Breach of promise doesn't pay as well as divorce and community property, but Dad thinks of it as paying the overhead. Divorce and community property is where he makes his Rolls-Royce money. With a reputation like his, he gets forty percent of the community property."

"What you're trying to tell me is that Miss Amanda Lewis is nothing more than a gold digger, is that what you're saying? That she doesn't love my father at all, and all she's really interested in is his money?"

"I'm not saying that at all. For all I know, your stewardess may be the exception that proves the rule. All I'm saying is that statistics, not to mention my father's Rolls-Royce, prove conclusively that once these romances get out of the airlines terminal they have a tendency to wind up in court. Generally, this happens when the stewardess realizes that Prince Charming is almost as old as her father. But sometimes it works the other way. Prince Charming suddenly realizes that he has temporarily gone insane. Like when he's with his stewardess and meets an old friend, and the old friend says, 'I didn't know you had a daughter.' "

"You're not talking about my father," I said. "My father's not like that. He's flying all over, all the time. He must have met two thousand stewardesses."

"*Stewardii*," Einstein corrected me. "Right. And he never got caught before, right?"

"Right."

"That's what worries Moose and me most about yours," Einstein said. "You must really have a smart one, to get to your father the way she has, after all the others tried and failed."

"If you're so smart," I said, "you tell me how she did that."

"She's playing on his sense of guilt, that's how," Einstein said.

"I don't quite follow you," I said.

"Every one of our parents feels guilty about our being in here," Einstein said. "And your stewardess was smart enough to figure that out. Psychologically speaking, Runt, your father is not only getting what he thinks will be his own private stewardess, but once they get married he can stop feeling sorry about your being in the orphanage."

"I'm not saying I agree with you one little bit, Einstein," I said. "But even if everything you say is true, what could I do about it?"

"We'll think of something, me and Moose," Einstein said. "Which brings us back to my feeling guilty about what we're doing to Moose. Here he is, worrying himself sick about your stewardess, and here you are, doing your best to make a fool out of him."

"I don't really see how letting Moose get to be a football hero is making a fool out of him, Einstein," I said. "Particularly when the alternative is you and me and Number Three all dressed up in lion suits. Talk about being made a fool of!"

"You've got a point, I suppose," Einstein said. "Better a football hero than a cheerleader in a lion suit."

Chapter 9

What I thought about on the way back to the cell was that while I didn't necessarily agree with Einstein and Moose that my father was suffering from a bad case of infatuation, Grandfather did. The only time I had known Grandfather to be wrong about anything was about politics. Just before an election, Grandfather would announce that he refused to believe that people would be so stupid as to elect the politicians who wound up getting elected. My father getting married to Miss Amanda Lewis wasn't exactly politics, and Grandfather, who was obviously upset about it, might be right this time.

119

When I got to the cell, Moose and The Thing were having a tug of war with the football The Thing had caught someplace.

"What were you and Four-Eyes talking about?" Moose asked.

"Nothing special," I said. "But I did have an interesting talk with Coach Ramsey. About the go-cart racing."

"What did he have to say?" Moose asked.

"He said he thought you might want to race against some of the guys on the football team," I said.

Moose thought that over for a minute.

"That would sure be better than racing against you and Number Three," he said.

"There's one little condition," I said.

"Let's hear it," Moose said.

"He also thinks it would be nice if you tossed the ball around with the team on Wednesday and Thursday," I said.

"What for?"

"Oh, so you could get to know them, I suppose," I said. "That might come in handy during the game."

"All they're going to have to do is let me have the ball and get out of my way," Moose said. "I don't have to know them for them to do that."

"Well," I said desperately, "it would give you a chance to tell them that before the go-cart race."

"You may have a point, Runt," he said. "Okay. I'll go." He started toward the door. "Well, let's go!"

"Go where?"

"Out to lay out the go-cart racecourse you were talking about. I want to practice."

"It's a little dark for that now, Moose," I said. "It's half-past eight. I don't think we could see well enough to put the flags out."

He thought about that a minute. "Okay," he said. "We'll do it tomorrow, right after last class. Then I'll race against you and Number Three. Feinberg can be the starter."

"Right," I said.

"Sit down, and we'll play some chess," he said.

"I don't know how to play chess, I'm afraid," I said.

"Sit down," Moose said, "and I'll teach you." He put his hand on my shoulder. I sat down. It was either that or get both legs broken. Actually, learning about chess wasn't as bad as I would have thought. In fact, it was sort of interesting. When I told Moose that I found it interesting, he said he wasn't surprised, that he thought it would appeal to someone with a devious mind like mine.

We went directly from our last class the next day to the track. Moose watched as Einstein and I put the flags out and Number Three got the go-carts out and gassed them up. It was, of course, against the rules to take the go-carts out on the campus, but there was nothing that could be done about that. Moose was determined to practice, and I was in no position to tell him he couldn't.

I tried to think of pleasant things, like how pretty the flags looked stuck in the grass, marking off the course. It didn't look much like a possible tulip bed, unless you wanted a narrow winding tulip bed about half a mile long, but the flags looked pretty, flapping in the breeze.

We got the engines going and the go-carts lined up side by side. Einstein Feinberg tied his handkerchief to a stick and waved it at us. Moose stepped on his gas pedal as hard as he could. The engine roared. Moose started to move off, hunched over his steering wheel. I pushed on my gas pedal just hard enough to make the clutch catch and went around Moose as if he was standing still. I took my foot off the gas and Number Three raced around me, and then slowed as he took his foot off his gas pedal, too.

Moose slowly passed us, his engine racing as fast as it would go. Number Three looked at me. We both knew what was wrong. Moose outweighed us by at least 120 pounds. The engine was barely powerful enough to move him at all. There was no way that Moose was going to be able to win a race unless the people he was racing against really put their hearts into cheating. The only way Number Three and I could keep from passing Moose was by driving in little jumps. You know what I mean — give it just enough gas to get it moving and then stop it until he catches up and passes you, and then do the same thing again.

Not only were the guys on the football team not going to be able to figure out how to do that when he raced against them, but they wouldn't even want to. Coach Ramsey had brainwashed them into accepting his philosophy of sportsmanship: "It matters not how you play the game, but whether or not you win." The guys on the football team would go around Moose and leave him far behind, and he wasn't going to like that at all.

But there was nothing to do now but keep it up. Moose rolled slowly down the hill toward the lake, and Number Three and I kept behind him, mainly by stepping on the brake pedal a lot.

We were so busy doing this that we didn't see Mr. Davis until he came rolling down the racecourse after us on his professional-model grounds sweeper. He caught up with me first.

"What are you guys doing with go-carts in Mrs. Ludwell's tulip beds?" he shouted at me from up on top of the sweeper.

I stopped my go-cart and waited for him to get off his sweeper. I looked up at it. There it was again.

The little metal tag on the engine: 7.5 horsepower. Seven-point-five–horsepower was almost twice as powerful as the engines in the go-carts.

"Now, what's going on here?" Mr. Davis asked.

"I guess we got lost," I said.

"What do you mean, lost?" Mr. Davis asked. "You know you're not supposed to take those go-carts out on the campus!"

"We'll take them right back in," I said.

"You'd better," he said. "You know how fussy Mrs. Ludwell is about her tulip beds."

"I've been admiring your professional-model grounds sweeper," I said. "Aren't you afraid that someone's going to steal it?"

"No way you can steal it," he said, "if that's what you're thinking, Pete Peters, and knowing you it probably is. When I put it away at night, I run a heavy chain through the wheels."

I looked up ahead. Number Three had seen Mr. Davis. I don't know what he said to Moose Hanrahan, but they had left the possible tulip bed and were driving as fast as they could back toward the track-and-field arena. As fast as they could wasn't very fast, not as long as Number Three let Moose go first.

What we should have done, I suppose, is walked around the go-cart racecourse before the race was actually run. But we didn't. For one thing, we were pretty busy on Wednesday and Thursday. Moose said that if he had to practice football, we would have to go with him to keep him company and help him and Einstein Feinberg play chess. Having to practice was bad enough, Moose said, without having to be bored, too.

Einstein Feinberg set up the chessboard in the grandstand. Whenever he made a move, he would tell us what it was. People who play chess have a sort of code. Queen's Pawn to Queen Three, for example, means you move the pawn in front of the queen out one space.

So when Einstein made a move, either Number Three or I would run out on the field to where Moose was throwing the ball around or tackling the other guys on the team and give him the message: "Queen's Pawn to Queen Three."

Moose's eyes would sort of glass over. He was carrying the whole game in his head, you see. Then he would say something like, "King's Bishop to Queen Five." That was his move. And either Number Three or I would then run off the field to the grandstand and tell Einstein Feinberg, who would move the chess piece on the board. Then Einstein would make his move, and one of us would run out and tell Moose what it was.

Number Three and I got more exercise than Moose did.

Coach Ramsey didn't like it much, seeing us running on and off the field, but he didn't say anything. He just stood on the sidelines wearing a smile as he watched Moose throw the ball around. He didn't even say anything when Moose threw a ball a little too fast for the receiver to catch and the receiver stopped it with his face. I knew what he was thinking. What's a little bloody nose compared to breaking Ludwell's unbroken record of lost football games?

Thursday night Number Three and I were very busy, from midnight until breakfast on Friday. Swapping engines around between a go-cart and a professional-model grounds sweeper isn't as easy as it might sound. It's not just a matter of unbolting one and taking it out and then putting the other one in. You have to disconnect fuel lines and control lines and drive belts, and that's not very easy to do by the light of a flashlight, especially if you have to work right under where someone is sleeping.

Once we thought we were caught for sure. Mr. Davis made a blood-chilling noise inside his apartment, and I thought we were finished. After a minute, though, I remembered that my mother's doctor made noises like that when he was snoring. It turned out that that was what Mr. Davis was doing.

Getting rid of Mr. Davis on Friday was a stroke of genius, even if I do say so myself. If he showed up around what he thought of as Mrs. Ludwell's possible tulip beds and saw Moose and two other guys racing around it on go-carts, he was going to cause trouble. And when we got out of the last class, I saw that he had every intention of being around. He was up on top of his professional-model grounds sweeper, headed toward the lake. He had a puzzled look on his face, and I thought I knew why.

"Hi there, Mr. Davis," I said, catching up with him and the sweeper. "Something wrong with your sweeper?"

"Doesn't seem to have any power," he grumbled.

"That's funny," I said. "It says right there on the engine block that it's a seven-point-five–horsepower engine. You'd think a seven-point-five–horsepower engine would run that thing faster than that, wouldn't you?"

"They don't make things the way they used to," he said. "Piece of junk, that's what this is!"

"I don't suppose you've thought about loading it up on the pickup truck and taking it back to the dealer, have you?" I asked.

"I was just thinking about doing that," he said.

I helped him load it on the truck. That made him even madder. The go-cart engine wouldn't even pull the sweeper up the ramp into the back of the truck. It took all we had to push it on. He told me he was going to give the dealer a piece of his mind, and I bet he did.

The race went off more or less as scheduled. Coach

Ramsey was determined that Moose should get beaten, so he picked two of the smallest guys on the team to race against him. He had figured out how heavy Moose was, and that the same engine, as the go-carts were supposed to have, would carry smaller guys faster than it would carry a big guy.

But when Coach Ramsey blew his whistle and the three of them started off, things were more or less evened out, because the go-carts were evenly matched. The two little guys on go-carts with 3.5-horsepower engines were just about as fast as Moose on his go-cart with the 7.5-horsepower engine from Mr. Davis's professional-model grounds sweeper.

As soon as the race started Moose pulled ahead of the other two go-carts. It was sort of downhill at the starting line, and that gave Moose an advantage. Coach Ramsey looked baffled. He thought he had everything arranged so that the football guys were going to win fair and square, because they were smaller than Moose, and here Moose was leading the race.

Then they got to the part of the course where it went up a little hill, and that put Moose at a disadvantage, because even with a 7.5-horsepower engine, there was a lot of Moose to move uphill. The football-team guys both passed him before he got to the top of the hill, and Coach Ramsey started to smile again.

But then it was downhill, and downhill was

Moose's thing. He passed the other two go-carts again, and smiled and waved at them as he did so.

And then, all of a sudden, the two guys from the football team drove into the lake, and that ended the race. They didn't sink out of sight or anything, because the water wasn't that deep there. It didn't come up any higher than their waists, but the engines were underwater, and stopped.

I thought for a minute that they had done it on purpose, but when we ran over and saw how mad they were, I knew that wasn't the case. What we finally figured out had happened was that Mr. Davis had gone to Mrs. Ludwell and asked her where she wanted her tulip beds.

She had been a little confused at first, but after Mr. Davis had told her that Number Three had been involved, she decided that her loving boy was planning a little surprise for her. So she went down to the possible tulip beds and looked them over. Everything was just about perfect, she said, but she thought it would look very nice if the tulip bed went right down to the water's edge.

She moved the flags that way.

Moose, of course, had been over the course before and knew where to go. What had happened was that when he had passed the two football guys and waved at them, he hadn't bothered to look at the flags. If he had looked, of course, they wouldn't have been there, but he didn't look, and that was what counted. He kept driving where he thought the course was. The guys from the football team drove where the flags told them to drive. Right into the lake.

This didn't please Coach Ramsey, of course. No football coach likes to see his players doing something dumb like driving a go-cart into a lake, and he immediately started shouting about sportsmanship and unfair tactics and demanded a rematch.

There was no way we could run the race over that day. Getting the go-carts out of the lake was going to be a problem, and even after we did get them out they would be all wet and would have to be dried out before they would run again.

Moose said that the race didn't count, but he was reasonable about it. We could do it again, after the Barton Academy football game. He would play in the game anyway. He had made a deal, he said, and he would live up to it, even if that meant he would have to go on the field with a pair of dummies who had driven into the lake.

Saturday, the day of the game, began with a very unusual occurrence. About ten minutes to seven, just before breakfast, Junior Ludwell showed up in our room. What I thought at first was that he had come up there to catch us in bed instead of taking a bath and making the beds, as the schedule called for us to be doing.

But that wasn't it at all. He didn't say a word about our still being in bed. He had other things on his mind. For one thing, he had had a telephone call from Dr. Brooks, the headmaster of Barton Academy, the night before. Junior Ludwell said that information had reached Dr. Brooks that certain elements of the Barton student body planned to make off with the bronze bust of our beloved founder, Number Three's grandfather, James Foxcroft Ludwell, Sr., from where it sat in the William C. Emmons Memorial Library. Junior Ludwell said that he couldn't imagine what they were thinking of. Neither could I. If I were going to steal a statue, I think I'd steal one of a naked lady, not one of just the head and shoulders of an old guy with a beard.

But Junior Ludwell was determined, he said, that there should not be an incident to mar what he said he was sure was going to be a day the Ludwell School would long remember. He was talking about our beating Barton Academy and breaking the twenty-two-year run of losses. He wanted to remove the temptation, he said. What he meant was that he had told Mr. Davis to bring the pickup truck over to the library, and what he wanted us to do was help load Number Three's grandfather's bust into the pickup truck. Mr. Davis would then drive it over to the stadium and lock it up in one of the underneath storage rooms with steel doors. Afterward we would bring it back to the library.

"And after you have helped Mr. Davis, Monroe," Junior Ludwell said, "Mrs. Ludwell and I would be happy if you would take breakfast with us at Head-master's House."

"We're invited for breakfast, Pop?" Number Three asked. He was as surprised as we were.

"No, just Monroe," Junior Ludwell said. "You and Peters will eat with the other boys at the special brunch we are going to share with our guests."

"What special brunch?" Number Three asked.

"Instead of breakfast at seven and lunch at twelve, we're having a special brunch at eleven, when the boys from Barton get here," Junior Ludwell said.

"Then how come, Pop, Moose gets to eat and we don't?"

"I've asked you time and again," Junior Ludwell replied, "please not to call me Pop."

"I don't think he wants anybody from Barton to see me until I show up on the field," Moose said. "Right?"

"Well," Junior Ludwell said, a little embarrassed. "I'll admit that thought did run through my mind."

"I'm not going to eat breakfast in Number Three's house unless he gets invited," Moose said. "And Runt Peters, too. No way."

"James," Ludwell Junior said, caving in, "I'm sure that your mother would love to have you and Rutherford join us for breakfast."

"Thanks," Number Three said.

"Before you come over, make sure you've got your shaggy dog locked up in a storage room. I don't want to give Dr. Brooks an excuse to blame The Thing for Barton's taking a licking."

As it turned out, none of us got to eat in Headmaster's House. As Moose was carrying the bust of Number Three's grandfather out of the library to Mr. Davis's pickup truck, I saw something that really surprised me. It was a Rolls-Royce convertible, just like Einstein Feinberg's father's. I thought it was highly unlikely that it was Mr. Feinberg, particularly since it wasn't quite half-past seven in the morning. And then, all of a sudden, the Rolls skidded to a stop and backed up toward us.

It was Mr. Feinberg all right, but he wasn't driving. Grandfather was driving. Mr. Feinberg was just sitting there with a horrified look on his face. I had the feeling he wasn't too happy with Grandfather's driving.

Chapter 10

"Runt," Grandfather shouted at me, standing up on the seat, "you sure picked a fine time to steal Old Man Ludwell's statue."

"We're not stealing it, Grandfather," I said. "We're going to lock it up so that the guys from Barton Academy can't steal it."

"Rutherford," Mr. Feinberg said, "I would consider it a personal favor if you would discourage that splendid, if somewhat shaggy, animal of yours from getting in the car."

The Thing, who really likes Grandfather, was already at the car getting ready to jump in.

"Don't do that!" Moose boomed. "Come back here to Moose and be a good puppy!" Truth, as I say, being stranger than fiction, The Thing did just that.

"You must be J. Monroe Hanrahan," Mr. Feinberg said, getting out of the car. "Stanley has told me all about you."

"I'm glad to see that you got together with Mr. Peters," Moose said, shaking his hand.

"What's going on?" I asked. "Grandfather, what are you doing here?"

"I'll tell you that just as soon as you tell me what you're really doing with Old Man Ludwell's statue," he said.

"We're going to lock it up with The Thing in one of the storerooms, so that Barton Academy can't steal it," I said.

"Well, hurry up and get it over with," Grandfather said, still not telling me what was going on. "And meet us back at your room." He looked at Mr. Feinberg. "Get in the car, Feinberg," he said. "We don't have any time to waste."

Mr. Feinberg got in the car and both of them drove off.

We put Mr. Ludwell, Sr.'s bust in the storeroom, hung a DANGER WILD ANIMAL DO NOT ENTER sign on it, pushed The Thing inside, and closed the door after him. Then we went back to the cell.

Everybody was there. By everybody, I mean that

Einstein Feinberg, Mr. Feinberg, and Grandfather were there when we walked in, and before anybody could say anything Ludwell Junior and Coach Ramsey, both of them a little out of breath from running up the stairs, came in.

"Thank God, we're in time!" Coach Ramsey said.

"Mr. Peters," Junior Ludwell said, puffing a lot, "there seems to be a little misunderstanding."

"What kind of a misunderstanding, Lushwell?" Grandfather asked.

"And how are you today, Mr. Feinberg?" Junior Ludwell said to Einstein's father, shaking his hand. Then he turned back to Grandfather. "The office tells me that you're taking Rutherford and Monroe and Stanley to Florida, Mr. Peters," he said. "Surely you can't be serious."

"Never more serious in my life," Grandfather said. "And I'm glad you're here, Lushwell. We want to take your boy, little Lushwell the Third, with us, too."

"You can have your grandson, Mr. Peters," Coach Ramsey said. "And you can have Junior Ludwell's kid, but you're not taking *my* Moose Hanrahan anywhere!"

"Give him the authorization, Feinberg," Grandfather said to Mr. Feinberg.

Mr. Feinberg handed Junior Ludwell a sheet of paper with a gold seal and a little ribbon stuck to it.

"You will find that in perfect legal order, Mr. Ludwell," Mr. Feinberg said. "I made it up myself. It's an authorization from Mr. Hanrahan for Mr. Peters to take Monroe to Florida. He was very understanding under the circumstances."

"What are you talking about?" Coach Ramsey demanded.

"Mr. Hanrahan once had a disastrous stewardess experience himself," Mr. Feinberg said.

"I don't understand what the problem is," Grandfather said to Junior Ludwell. "We'll have the boys back in time for class on Monday."

"You don't understand what the problem is?" Coach Ramsey sort of shouted. "You want to take the only Ludwell Lion who can run twenty-five yards without tripping over his shoelaces to Florida, and you ask me what the problem is?"

"What Coach Ramsey is saying, Mr. Peters," Junior Ludwell explained, "is that we have an important football game today, I might say a *very* important football game today. The Ludwell School, in other words, needs Moose. I mean, Monroe."

"Not as much as my infatuated son needs him," Grandfather said. "Moose is very important to our plan of action."

"You can't have him, and that's that!" Coach Ramsey said. "In other words, you can have him over my dead body!"

"If that's the way it has to be, Baldy," Grandfather said, putting up his fists, "so be it!"

"Gentlemen, gentlemen," Mr. Feinberg said, getting between them. "I'm sure there is room for reason and negotiation."

The way it worked out was that we would stick around long enough for Moose to play football. In exchange for that, Junior Ludwell said that we could take Number Three with us, too, even if he didn't know how he was going to explain it to Mrs. Ludwell.

Everything went pretty smoothly after that. We all, except Junior Ludwell and Coach Ramsey, got in Mr. Feinberg's car and went off campus to get something to eat. I don't think that Coach Ramsey, who is always concerned with proper nutrition and things like that, would have liked it very much if he knew we had a hundred-percent junk-food breakfast at Pasquale's Sloppy Taco Palace, but as Grandfather pointed out to Mr. Feinberg, what Coach Ramsey didn't know couldn't hurt him, and Grandfather personally believed we were at least as smart as The Thing, who wouldn't eat anything that was bad for him.

We went to the stadium just in time for Moose to get dressed for the game. The minute Barton Academy's coach, Mr. Stevens, and Dr. Brooks, Barton's headmaster, saw Moose come lumbering out onto the field, they started making a fuss. They said that Moose was clearly a ringer, which is what they call football players who aren't what they seem to be.

But Junior Ludwell had expected something like that. He had certified copies of Moose's birth certificate saying he was two weeks shy of being fourteen years old, and a letter from where Moose had gone to school before he came to Ludwell saying that Moose had never played varsity football there, so he still had all his eligibility.

Einstein explained that eligibility business to me. He said that in the old days, when some high schools got a football player like Moose — the kind that comes along once in maybe twenty years, the kind that really helps them set records — they were reluctant to see them graduate and leave. So they set things up so the really good football players could spend five, six, even seven years in high school. It got so bad that the authorities had made a rule saying you can only play high-school football for four years. Otherwise, some football players would be a whole lot older than other football players, and it wouldn't be fair.

The game got off to a slow start. Barton won the toss and elected to receive. Moose kicked off. The first ball he kicked exploded, and they had to do it again. The second ball he kicked went over the fence at the end of the stadium into the parking lot, and while they were getting him another one, three of Barton's tackles and their quarterback went to Coach Stevens and tried to resign.

But by half-time the score was Barton 0, Ludwell 52, and it looked as if we had a pretty good chance to win. I had never seen Coach Ramsey really smile before. He looked like a certain politician Grandfather was absolutely positive couldn't win, either.

The second half began with Barton kicking off to us. Frog-Eyes Davis caught it, and probably because he was our pre-Moose version of a football hero and was a little discouraged because Moose had made all of the touchdowns so far, he disobeyed the game plan.

The game plan had two versions. Version One said give the ball to Moose and let him score touchdowns. Version Two said that if somehow somebody besides Moose got his hands on the ball, he was to stand where he was until Moose could run interference for him, and then he could score the touchdown himself. Version Two was sort of the emergency game plan.

Well, Frog-Eyes had liked being a football hero, scoring touchdowns without help, so when he caught the ball, he started charging up the field without waiting for Moose to run interference for him.

He got maybe thirty yards when ten of the eleven guys on the Barton team jumped on him.

That made it first down and ten to go.

Moose understood what Frog-Eyes had wanted to do. (Coach Ramsey didn't. He was jumping up and down on the sidelines screaming at Frog-Eyes for not following the game plan.) So, in the huddle, when the quarterback started to tell them what the next play was going to be, Moose told him to shut up.

"What we're going to do," Moose said, "is I'm going to throw a pass to Frog-Eyes. The rest of you run downfield with him and keep the Barton wimps away from him."

"But if we're all downfield, who's going to protect you?" the quarterback asked.

"I told you once to shut up," Moose replied. "I'm not going to tell you again."

So the ball was centered to Moose, and the rest of the team formed a circle around Frog-Eyes, and they ran downfield.

Well, you have to give credit where credit is due, and the Barton Buffalos really showed they had guts. About six of them went charging down the field to tackle Moose before he could throw his pass to Frog-Eyes. Moose was all alone.

It took all six of them a long time to catch Moose, who had to wait until Frog-Eyes and the other nine guys got down the field so Frog-Eyes could catch his pass when he threw it. But finally the six Barton guys sort of cornered Moose by the sideline. They kept jumping on him, trying to tackle him, or at least knock him down, and he kept swatting them off, and they would shake themselves and then jump on him again. That's what I mean about their having guts.

That's when The Thing got in the game. Apparently what happened is that the guys from Barton who were determined to steal Old Man Ludwell's statue either decided that the DANGER WILD ANIMAL DO NOT ENTER sign we had hung over the storeroom was a phony, or they were determined to see inside anyway.

The minute they opened the door The Thing came running out. He didn't bite any of the guys who opened the door. He was all excited by the noise he heard coming from the field. He just knocked them out of the way and went to see what all the fuss was about.

Well, you can hardly blame The Thing for what happened. How was he supposed to know it was all just clean sportsmanship? All he saw was six guys jumping all over Moose, and Moose swatting them away. He did what any loyal dog would do when he saw a friend under attack.

Despite all the screaming, nobody got really hurt. They were wearing all that protective equipment, and while The Thing made a mess of that, I'm willing to admit, it was too thick for his teeth to get through. The only thing that got punctured, in other words, was the football itself.

But after a scrimmage with The Thing, there was no way Coach Stevens could talk eleven guys (any eleven guys, not just the guys on the football team) into going out on the field, so what they had to do was forfeit the game.

As soon as that was settled, we all got in Mr. Feinberg's car — The Thing, too, since Grandfather said that not only had he earned a trip, but, now that Grandfather thought of it, he was embarrassed he hadn't thought of taking him along before. Then we went out to the airport, where Grandfather had one of the company planes waiting for us. It was a little plane, and the pilot said that with Moose and The Thing on board there was no way he could get it off the ground. So Mr. Feinberg stayed behind.

When we got to Florida, we had a little trouble getting out of the airport. Grandfather had to go to the gentlemen's rest facility, and when he didn't meet us right away to get in the cab, I went to look for him. I got there just in time to keep two cops and two guys in white coats from pushing him onto a bus. The bus had a sign reading, GREATER MIAMI BEACH 80-PLUS SENIOR CITIZENS SCENIC TOURS.

It turned out that what had happened was that when he came out of the gentlemen's rest facility, he must have been deep in thought, which sometimes makes him close his eyes and frown. The two guys in white coats were at the moment escorting the Greater Miami Beach 80-Plus Senior Citizens out of the airport after their scenic tour of it, and they naturally thought he was one of theirs.

After what Grandfather called them, they'll be more careful in the future, I'm sure, and I'm sure the cop Grandfather kicked in the stomach will think twice before taking the word of some guy just because he's wearing a white coat with "Geriatric Attendant" stitched on it.

After that, of course, Grandfather needed what he called "a little something to steady his nerves." The man in the South Seas Saloon, where Grandfather told the cab to stop, started to say something about not wanting any dogs or kids in his place of business, but then The Thing growled a little at him, and instead he gave us a handful of quarters to play the video games in the lobby while Grandfather was steadying his nerves inside the place. Grandfather said he was sure we had learned all about the natives of the South Seas in school and really didn't want to see the ladies doing the native dances inside on the bar.

We were there about an hour, I guess, before Grandfather came out. I could tell his nerves were steady. His face had its color back, and he was snapping his fingers in time to the music.

Then we went to the funeral home. Grandfather said that my father hadn't actually signed the papers yet to buy the place, but that the real-estate man had told him to move in for a week and see how he liked it.

It was bigger even than it had looked in the pictures. It was so big that my father couldn't even hear the doorbell when we rang it. I was afraid that maybe nobody was home, and was just about to say something when The Thing, who we naturally had on a leash, smelled food and started dragging me around the side of the house.

My father was home all right. The reason he hadn't heard the doorbell was because he was about to sit down to eat by the side of the swimming pool. Miss Amanda Lewis, who had apparently got a couple of days off from being a passenger comforts coordinator again, was with him. They were all dressed up for the occasion, and it was pretty obvious they hadn't expected to see anybody else, much less all of us.

The first thing that happened was that when Miss Amanda Lewis saw The Thing coming through the palm trees, barking happily at what he thought was going to be his supper, she stood up, screamed, and then took a couple of steps backward. If she hadn't been standing right on the edge of the swimming pool, that would have been the end of it. But that's the way things happen sometimes, and there she was, in the ten-foot six-inch deep part of the pool in her cocktail dress, with my father using the language my mother said he got from Grandfather and the other dirty old men at the Athletic Club.

Moose, who had earned a First-Class Lifesaving Badge at camp, but who had never before had a chance to use it, kicked off his shoes, jumped in after her, and dragged her down to the shallow end by her hair, which is what they had taught him the rescuer was supposed to do if the rescuee was hysterical.

When Moose jumped in, there was no way to keep The Thing out, so he jumped in, too, and since I had his leash wrapped around my wrist so he couldn't get away, that meant I was in there, too.

When Moose got Miss Amanda Lewis to the shallow end of the pool, he picked her up and then threw her over his shoulder, in what they call the fireman's carry. I knew that what he was going to do was carry her someplace and give her artificial respiration, but she didn't know that and started to scream even louder than she had been about her ruined hair and dress.

My father told Moose that Miss Amanda Lewis didn't need artificial respiration, and that he should have been able to figure that out himself from all the noise she was making. Anyway, Moose handed her to my father, and my father took her in the house.

The Thing then went over to the table where Grandfather was steadying his nerves some more with one of the three bottles of champagne my father and Miss Amanda Lewis were going to have with their dinner. I knew what was on The Thing's mind, and so did Grandfather. He socked The Thing on the nose, and then yelled at all of us:

"If you guys want any of this, you'd better hurry!"

We were all a little hungry, but Moose most of all, after the way he'd rescued Miss Amanda Lewis from the pool, so what happened was that when Miss Amanda Lewis, in a very attractive dress but with her hair still all wet, came back out to the side of the pool, there wasn't anything left of the ham but the bone The Thing was gnawing.

The first thing we learned was that she hadn't had the opportunity to tell my father she didn't like dogs. From the way The Thing growled at her, it went both ways.

"Get that damned dog away from me!" she sort of screamed at my father when The Thing growled at her.

"He thinks you're trying to steal his bone," Grandfather said. "I don't *think* it's anything personal."

"I am sure, Father," my father said, in that tone of voice he uses when he is really upset, "that there is some perfectly good reason for your being here."

Grandfather said that he had heard so much about the place he just had to come down and have a look for himself.

"Since the Runt's going to be living here," he said, "I wanted to take a real good look at it."

"If you'll tie that *lovely* dog up somewhere," Miss Amanda Lewis said, in the kind of voice she must have used when she was a passenger comforts coordinator, "I'd just *love* to show Rutherford and his *darling* little friends around."

So Miss Amanda Lewis showed us around the place. Grandfather was even more enthusiastic about the place than Moose was, and Moose was really enthusiastic about it. Moose told my father that he had never seen, as long as he'd been around the profession, any place that was more just naturally suited to be a funeral home.

"I'm sure you meant that as a compliment," Miss Amanda Lewis said.

"I'm really going to like it around here," Moose said.

Miss Amanda Lewis's eyebrows went up when he said that, but she didn't say anything. She decided to be a gracious hostess.

"Now, was that eight-pound ham enough for everybody, or is anybody still hungry?"

"I am," Moose said.

I thought that after Miss Amanda Lewis got to know Moose better, she would know better than to ask him a question like that.

And then Grandfather spoke up: "I'm starved," he said. "I guess those three Coconut Surprises I had at the South Seas Saloon gave me an appetite."

"Now that you mention it," Number Three said.

"Me, also," Einstein Feinberg said.

"I guess I could eat a little something," I said.

"Well," Miss Amanda Lewis said, "since we didn't expect you, I'm afraid there's not much else here."

"There's not?" Grandfather said, shocked.

Miss Amanda Lewis said she'd be happy to run out and get us all some Kentucky Fried Chicken. Grandfather said that he was surprised to hear her say that, that he was surprised to hear a woman who wanted a young boy to come live with her say she wanted to feed him junk food. He said he was surprised that she didn't know what young people like me and old people like him needed was home-cooked food, and that if she expected us to come live with her, she'd have to learn how to cook.

"Live with us?" Miss Amanda Lewis said, very politely. "I'm not sure I completely understand what you mean by that."

So Grandfather told her what he meant. He said

that with a house this big, it just made sense to fill it up, and besides he was tired of living in the Athletic Club anyway.

About that time, The Thing got loose from where Moose had tied him to a tree. I could have told Moose that a rope wouldn't hold The Thing long, that he chewed right through ropes, and that it took a chain if you really wanted to keep him someplace.

"Speaking of The Thing, Rutherford," Ludwell Three said, as he and Einstein Feinberg tried to pull The Thing away from the ladder to the high dive. Miss Amanda Lewis had run up there when she saw The Thing was loose. The Thing probably thought she was hiding something to eat from him. He only growls like the way he was growling when it's connected with food. "We have a little announcement to make."

"What kind of announcement?" I asked.

"Moose and I and Einstein have decided that what we're going to give you as a going-away present when you come here to live is The Thing."

"Over my dead body!" Miss Amanda Lewis screamed from the high dive. "I won't have that ferocious beast in *my* house . . ."

"Every growing boy needs a dog," Grandfather said. "I'm surprised you don't know that."

"We'll miss him, of course," Moose said. "But he'll be here every time we come to see you, Runt. Say once a month, and every holiday, and during the summer vacations."

Moose finally went over to the high dive and picked up The Thing and made him sit in his lap.

"I can't hear a thing," he announced. "The way he's barking at her."

With Moose holding The Thing on his lap, Miss Amanda Lewis felt safe to come off the high dive. She sort of ran over to my father and asked him for the keys to his car. He gave them to her, and she left.

At first we thought she'd gone out to the grocery store to buy something to cook for us to eat, but then she called up from the airport and told my father she had had some second thoughts about assuming the responsibilities of marriage and wanted some time to think it over. So far as I know that was the last time he ever heard from her.

Moose's father took the funeral home off my father's hands, and it's now called Hanrahan's Southern Funeral Hacienda. The apartment that was supposed to be mine is now Moose's, and we're all going to spend the summer with him there, instead of at Camp Gitcheegoomee. Mr. Hanrahan, Mr. Feinberg, and Grandfather are going to come down from the city to be with us, and we hope my father will be able to get there too, from wherever he happens to be at the time. Mrs. Feinberg says she'll make him a home-cooked meal, and that just may get him to come.

γ